A VICTIM FOR THE SACRIFICE

A hot steel band tightened around the boy's chest. He had to close his eyes and fight for breath at the horror of the memory. "This terrible place," he whispered.

"Where was it?"

"Underground. A mine. No, it was a tunnel. It was very old. I think it's always been there."

"What happened when you went in there?"

"A sacrifice."

"Someone died?" the priest asked.

"Yes. Someone. A good friend."

"Who killed this person?"

The boy slowly opened his eyes. "They did."

Books by Christopher Pike

BURY ME DEEP
CHAIN LETTER 2: THE ANCIENT EVIL
DIE SOFTLY
THE ETERNAL ENEMY
FALL INTO DARKNESS
FINAL FRIENDS #1: THE PARTY
FINAL FRIENDS #2: THE DANCE
FINAL FRIENDS #3: THE GRADUATION
GIMME A KISS
LAST ACT
MASTER OF MURDER
MONSTER
REMEMBER ME
ROAD TO NOWHERE
SCAVENGER HUNT
SEE YOU LATER
SPELLBOUND
WHISPER OF DEATH
WITCH

Available from ARCHWAY Paperbacks

Christopher Pike

Scavenger Hunt

AN ARCHWAY PAPERBACK
Published by POCKET BOOKS

New York   London   Toronto   Sydney   Tokyo   Singapore

AN ARCHWAY PAPERBACK *Original*

An Archway Paperback published by
POCKET BOOKS, a division of Simon & Schuster Inc.
1230 Avenue of the Americas, New York, NY 10020

ISBN: 0-671-73686-8

First Archway Paperback printing July 1989

15   14   13   12   11   10

AN ARCHWAY PAPERBACK and colophon are
registered trademarks of Simon & Schuster Inc.

Printed in the U.S.A.

IL 9+

FOR SHARON

PROLOGUE

In the Church

A VICTIM FOR THE SACRIFICE.

At last the boy understood what they wanted him for.

The church was old. It stood at the edge of the tiny run-down town, like a cathedral built in defiance of wind and dust, held fast by weed-choked desert and desperate night. The boy had spotted it from two miles away, the black silhouette of its crowning cross an outstretched hand of asylum pulling him toward it with pounding heart and weeping eyes. He needed a place to hide. They were coming.

He could *feel* them coming.

Yet the boy hesitated as he neared the top of the stone steps, his dry, gasping breath a hurricane in his ears. It was late. He didn't know if the church was open, and suddenly he couldn't bear the possibility that it might not be open. He thought that if he pulled on the door handle and it didn't budge, he'd begin to sob uncontrollably, or worse yet, begin to scream at the top of his lungs so that they would know where he was. Then it would finally be over. He wanted it to be over.

But that didn't mean he wanted to die. Not their way.

He had no choice. The people of the nearby town could not help him, even if they would open their doors to him. Only God could help him. He reached for the handle.

"Oh, sweet Jesus, please," he said.

It opened. Relief and cool air washed over him as he stepped inside. He smelled the wax of burning candles, sensed the silence of years of whispered prayers. Inside was almost as dark as outside. If not for the candles illuminating the altar, he would have stumbled on the vase of holy water set on top of a low pillar beside the doorway. He touched the water with the tip of his fingers as he tried vainly to moisten his cracked lips with his bone-dry tongue. He needed a drink in the worst way, but was reluctant to bend over and satisfy his thirst. The thought of germs didn't deter him; it was the fear of committing a blasphemy, especially now when he could ill afford to offend anybody. He blessed himself quickly and moved farther into the church.

The place was all but deserted. Only one old lady in black sat in a pew, and she stood quickly as he entered, throwing him a furtive glance and tightening her shawl over her hunched shoulders before disappearing into a wooden confessional booth built into a stone wall on the right side of the church. The boy relaxed slightly. There had to be a priest in the booth listening to confessions.

To the right of the main altar was a smaller shrine to the Virgin Mary. He had not been to church in years, but he remembered that Mother Mary was supposed to be especially good at protecting those in danger. Hurrying up the central aisle, he genuflected before the statue of the Madonna. He decided to say a prayer and light a candle. The Virgin had dozens of tiny candles burning at her feet already, their flames flickering drunkenly in small blue and red dishes above the flood of their own melted wax. The tiny flames irritated his already moist eyes, and he had to pull a handkerchief from his pocket to stop the tears from pouring over his cheeks.

A tarnished silver donation box sat to the side on the shrine. One was supposed to put something in it before lighting a candle, he recalled, and he searched his pants for change. He came up with two quarters. But before he slipped them in the box, he hesitated once more. To call the police, he would need at least one quarter, if not both of them. It would be foolish to throw away his money like this.

Then he remembered what he had seen, what he had heard with his own ears and felt with his two hands. He hastily slipped the money in the box and reached for the stick to light his candle.

Unfortunately, he couldn't get the thing to light. He couldn't get the wick to stand still. It kept moving, and he became angry with it until he realized it was his hands that were trembling. He had to grab his right wrist with his left palm to steady his hand sufficiently to make contact with the wick.

His candle lit, the boy turned his eyes up to the

Virgin. She was beautiful, and the sight of her soft face momentarily allowed him to blot out the horror of what was in his mind. He began to pray.

"Hail Mary, full of grace, the Lord is with thee. Blessed are thou amongst woman, and blessed is the fruit of thy womb, Jesus. Holy Mary, mother of God, pray for us sinners, now and at the hour of our death. Amen."

He repeated the prayer a dozen times, then another dozen, and at the end felt somewhat better. He left the shrine for a seat in a pew near the rear of the church. He needed to sit down, to rest, and he wanted to be near the door in case anyone approached. But he wondered if he had in fact been followed, if he wasn't just imagining things. He had to ask himself if they would dare enter a church, if they wouldn't explode in flames at the sight of a crucifix. The idea of being in a divinely protected place gave him some comfort.

Still, his hands continued to tremble.

The old lady in black was in the confessional booth a long time. When she came out she did not kneel to do her penance. A quick glance at him and she headed for the door. He tried to smile as she passed, but she lowered her wrinkled face and frowned. He must look like hell. The moment she was gone, he stood and strode to the confessional booth.

The priest must have been anxious to leave. The boy thought he heard the father sigh as he opened the door to the booth and sat down inside. Of course the boy could not be sure. The priest sat on the other side of a translucent screen of woven cloth that rendered him an ill-defined shadow beneath a dim overhead light.

The boy didn't know if he was happy or sad that the priest couldn't see him, and vice versa. He decided it didn't matter, as long as the priest would listen to him and not demand that he leave.

One thing for sure, the boy was not happy about the interior of the booth. It was poorly lit, cramped, a claustrophobic's nightmare. The wood of the small seat was not merely hard; his backside seemed to bruise just sitting on it. It was only with the greatest effort that he was able to shut the door to the booth. He could have been shutting the lid to his own coffin. Right away he began to have trouble breathing, and had to fight to calm himself.

"Yes?" the priest said after a minute when the boy had not spoken. The priest had a Spanish accent, which was no wonder—the church wasn't far from the Mexican border. The priest also sounded old, and the boy hoped that was good. He coughed once and began to speak.

"Bless me, Father, for I have sinned. It has been years since my last confession. These are my sins." He took a breath. "I've killed someone."

"What?" the priest asked, startled.

"I killed someone."

The priest paused. "Are you serious?"

"Yes, Father, I'm very serious."

His tone must have been convincing. The priest leaned forward behind the screen; the boy could actually feel his breath on his own face. The priest had had alcohol with his dinner. "How old are you, son?" the priest asked softly.

"Eighteen."

"Who did you kill?"

"I can't say. I don't know. I mean, I do know, but it's not important."

"It's not important?"

It's the least of my problems right now, the boy thought.

Yet he quickly wondered if that were true. There might be a pattern of cause and effect in what was happening to him. But he doubted that a logical analysis was going to give it to him. Not unless he started with the assumption that he was home in bed having a nightmare.

He shifted uneasily in the compact cubicle, his right elbow bumping the chipped adobe wall on his right, the orange dust staining his already filthy shirt. It looked as if Spanish conquistadors might have erected the church hundreds of years ago. Suddenly the boy didn't feel so well hidden as he felt trapped. The priest was waiting for him to continue.

"It's not why I'm here," the boy said. "I'll explain in a minute. But first I need to ask you something. Do you believe in the devil?"

"I'm a priest."

"I know you're a priest. But a lot of priests these days—they say the devil is just symbolic and stuff like that. Like out of the Middle Ages, you know?"

"Why are you asking this?"

"Because it's important. I need to know."

"I believe in the devil," the priest said.

"Good."

The priest spoke gently. "What is your problem, son?"

The boy couldn't control them. The tears simply gushed out. He had to reach for his handkerchief once more. "I'm so afraid."

"Tell me."

The boy began to tell him.

CHAPTER

I

CARL TIMMONS HAD A DREAM THE MORNING OF THE scavenger hunt. It was the same dream he'd had on and off for the last year, and it was different. But it began as it usually did, and, as always, everything that happened felt as if it were happening for the first time.

He was with his best friend, Joe, and the two of them were kids again. They were riding tricycles up a dusty gully. Overhead, the sky was clear and the day was bright. They were having a great time, playing in the big outdoors together without a care in the world.

Up ahead of them, at the end of the gully, was a huge dam. Joe understood the whole concept of the dam pretty well. He said there must be a lot of water on the other side of it, maybe a lake, but Carl couldn't imagine it. On their side of the dam everything was so dry and dusty. Carl thought there was probably just more of the same on the other side, or maybe nothing at all. In reality, he didn't much care what was there. But Joe liked to talk about it as they rode along. The subject of dams interested him greatly.

They were riding for quite some time and didn't notice that the sky had begun to darken. Black clouds swept over their heads, blotting out the last traces of sunlight. Lightning and thunder followed, and it began to rain. But not on them. Only behind the dam. They could see the rain from a distance, coming down like a beaded curtain. Joe said they should go back right then. He was afraid that the dam would overflow, maybe even break. But Carl didn't feel the least fear. The dam was big and strong, he thought. He didn't see how a little rain could possibly bring it down. And now he had a change of heart. He wanted to peek on the other side, to see with his own eyes if there really was a lake there, to see if Joe was right and he was wrong. He insisted they ride on.

They hadn't gone far when a thick bolt of lightning cracked the sky directly above them, accompanied by a deafening clap of thunder. A putrid smell filled the air, not the usual ozone smell lightning brought, but the odor of burnt flesh. Then it began to rain on them. The ground turned to mud. Carl quickly changed his mind about the dam. Now he was as scared as Joe. They turned their tricycles around and started pedaling like mad.

Then the thing fell out of the sky. They didn't see it. They had their backs to the dam, and with the thick rain it was hard to keep their eyes clear. But they heard it. The thing fell behind the dam, and the crash of its landing was louder than the thunder had been. The bad smell worsened, and they pedaled harder. Carl was afraid to look around. But he did look, finally, when his wheels began to sink deep into the mud and his burning lungs began to fail and he felt he could not go on.

This was where things changed, although in this particular nightmare on this particular morning, Carl only sensed the change without understanding it. Ordinarily in his dream, he would see cracks forming in the dam, with ribbons of water spouting out. This would, in fact, usually be the end of the dream, although occasionally the dam would actually break and a cascade of water would pour down on him and Joe, and he would wake up screaming. This time the cracks were present, but the spouting water was not exactly water. It had a red tinge to it, and he thought the thing that had fallen into the water behind the dam must be bleeding. He froze for a moment staring at the gook, knowing full well that the thing must have been huge to have darkened the entire lake. He was a believer in the lake by this time.

Joe was pulling on Carl's shirt and screaming that they had to keep going. Carl could barely move, he was so scared. The bloody water caught up with them and began to flow around the tires of their tricycles and over their feet, staining their pants. Carl finally bore down and got his wheel moving again. Joe was stronger. He pulled several feet ahead of him, but continued to shout back frantic words of encouragement.

Joe was in such a hurry to get away from the dam that he didn't pay enough attention to where he was going.

The gully was fairly wide. Joe was bearing to the left, near the steep mud wall. At the moment, riding up the wall of the gully was out of the question, but they both knew that farther along the walls would level out and they would be able to escape. The problem was, they weren't going to have the chance to get much farther. Their tricycles weren't very fast, and Carl only had to look over his shoulder to know the tiny cracks in the dam were growing bigger and fatter. The red water started to swim over his pedals. The only hope, as Carl saw it, was to head for a small hill several yards to the side of the right embankment.

Carl called out to Joe, trying to communicate his idea. But Joe was too far ahead, already past the hill, oblivious to how close the dam was to collapsing. Joe couldn't hear him, and Carl didn't know what to do. He could go after Joe, get close enough to tell him his plan, and risk getting swept away himself, or else he could ride straight for the hill. He really did care for Joe. They were best friends. But he honestly didn't think he could get to Joe in time. The rain was coming down too hard. He was too tired. He didn't want to die. He turned the wheel of his tricycle toward the right embankment.

The sides of the hill, in the middle of the gully, were not so steep as the walls of the gully, but they were just as muddy. Several times Carl pedaled up two feet only to slip back three. Finally, though, he reached the top of the mound and was able to pause and catch his breath. It was only then that he realized Joe was as good as done for. The dam was coming apart in huge chunks, and Joe was ploughing through a shallow stream that was about to become a raging river.

"Joe!" Carl screamed.

Joe heard him this time. He stopped and glanced

over his shoulder in time to watch a narrow splinter in the lower center of the dam split into a gaping red wound. The right and left sides of the dam held only a moment before collapsing in an avalanche of foam. The lake swept toward them both.

They were some distance from the dam. When the brunt of the wave hit the hill Carl stood on, it had leveled out enough to leave him untouched—for the moment. But it showed Joe no mercy. Carl saw Joe raise his hands in horror, cry out Carl's name, before he was buried beneath the thunderous cascade. Joe's tricycle flipped into the air and Carl caught a blur of his friend's legs and arms. Then Joe was gone, and Carl hung his head in sorrow.

But matters were far from over. The hill he stood upon was eroding beneath the onslaught of the red flood. He had a minute, two at most, before the ground beneath him would collapse and he would be swept away. Yet the possibility of drowning was not what sent the fear deep into his heart. It was the thing he saw. The thing the lightning bolt had sent crashing down from the heavens. Burnt and bleeding, but not dead—merely confined to the earth for a while. A thing that could never bleed to death.

It was a monster. It had a shape similar to a flying lizard from a time before man, and claws like a creature from the bottom of a cold sea. But it was neither. It was worse. It was from the *outside.* Small and scared as he was, Carl could see that. He could see it in the thing's eyes. They were red and hot, and there were hard black dots in their centers that had no fathomable bottom, that led nowhere, and had no care except for its all-consuming hunger. It was a monster that devoured the living. Especially little boys, which it found particularly tasty. And riding the crest of its own bloody wave, it was heading straight for him. . . .

The phone woke Carl. He sat up with a start. His eyes snapped open. For an instant he saw a face superimposed over the blue wall of his bedroom. It was not the face of the monster in his nightmare. It was a human face, and yet it was just as horrible. Somehow it resembled the monster, and he recognized the face. But before he could call out the person's name, the image faded, and the phone beside his bed rang a second time and he reached for it.

"Hi, Carl, did I wake you?"

Carl woke up in a hurry, pushing the dream aside. It was Cessy. Someone he wouldn't have dared to call. "No, I'm up," he said, trying to clear his throat with the words. "How are you?"

Cessy giggled. Sexy Cessy. She could giggle all day and a boy wouldn't mind. "I did wake you. I'm sorry. But we just had to talk to you. The Partridge Club is having their scavenger hunt today. We wanted to get you on our team before someone else got you."

Carl could not believe his luck. He had talked to Cessy many times during the year, and she had always been nice to him, yet they had never gone beyond superficial chatter. He had been wondering how he could gather the nerve to ask her out before school ended next week. And here she was setting up the perfect opportunity. The hunt was supposed to last all day and the teams were to be small.

"That would be great," he said.

"Wonderful! Tom told me I could count on you."

Tom Barrett was a friend of his, probably his best friend now that Joe was dead. Tom talked to Cessy regularly, although he'd never shown a romantic interest in her. Cessy went on, "Would you like to speak to him?"

"He's at your house?"

"Yes. He's sitting here on the deck of the pool, watching me swim." Cessy giggled again. "I'm naked."

"Sounds like fun." Carl wished he could see through his friend's eyes. "Sure, put Tom on. I'll see you at school."

"You'll see me before then, Carl."

He heard a loud splash and started to get excited. Tom came on the line. "How's it going, buddy?" he asked.

"All right," Carl said. "I haven't got out of bed yet. How are you?"

It was the usual mundane question to ask, but because it was Tom, Carl listened closely for the answer. Tom had been hit hard in the head during a football game last fall. The blow had knocked him out cold for fifteen solid minutes. The doctors said he was all right—he still did well in school and all that—but he had a tendency to fall silent for long periods and to wander off. Carl knew he was overprotective of him, but felt that should be the worst of his faults. It didn't bother him that Tom was with Cessy and he wasn't.

Well, it didn't bother him much.

"I'm the same," Tom said.

"Is that good or bad?" Carl asked.

"I don't know."

"What are you doing at Cessy's house?"

"Hanging out."

"Is she really swimming naked?"

"I think so. You want to give us a ride to school?"

"You want me to come get you?"

"If you can," Tom said.

"No problem. Did you talk Cessy into asking me to be in her group for the scavenger hunt?"

"We should all be together."

"Are you in the group, too?" Carl asked.

"Yeah."

"Great. See you soon."

"All right," Tom said. "Goodbye."

Carl said so long and set the phone down. It was only then he realized that his shirt was soaked with sweat. The nightmare came back to him in a rush. Yet he couldn't really remember it all, except that it had been different from the usual one. There had been a dragon or a snake at the end. Boy, he must be losing it. The blasted thing had scared the hell out of him.

Carl didn't spend much energy analyzing the dream. He'd done that many times before, and Freud's worst pupil could have solved the riddle in a minute. The last summer he'd gone for a hike with Joe Travers deep into the desert. The weather had been fine when they'd set out, but late the first night a storm had caught them unawares. People had trouble believing him to this day, but Carl swore the sky dropped six inches on them in less than thirty minutes. It was like being caught in a hurricane in the middle of the Bermuda Triangle.

They were trying to cross through a gully to get to shelter when an old beaver's dam or something farther up the gully must have broken and a flood came down on them and washed Joe away. Carl barely made it to safety on the other side. He tried to save Joe. He dived in and swam after him. He even split his side open on a boulder trying. But even though the flood was fierce, he didn't honestly think Joe would drown. They were in the middle of the desert for Christsakes.

But Joe did drown, or smother, and that was a fact, although they didn't find his body until a few months later. The flood had buried him beneath a pile of dirt and dead shrubs, and the insects and the weather had gotten to him by the time a ranger stumbled across his fleshless finger, pointing through the sun-baked mud at the blazing sky. All that remained was a skeleton, but the coroner said it was Joe, no question.

So Carl had his nightmares, and didn't have to wonder why. Yet he continued to ask himself why the flood had just happened to come down upon them the instant they climbed into the gully. There weren't any beavers or beaver dams in the desert. There was nothing but sand and lizards.

Carl climbed out of bed and went into the bathroom and took a cold shower. The sizzling sun through his bedroom window had already told him that it was going to be hot.

When he had finished washing and was dressed, he stopped by the kitchen for something to eat. He doubted he'd find anything. His dad drove a truck long distance, and hadn't been home in a week. He didn't know what his mom did, but she hadn't been home in eight years. She sent money at Christmas, though—a few hundred bucks each time; he figured she must be doing all right. He had a liberal family life: he stayed out of his dad's way and his dad stayed out of his and they got along fine. He took care of himself. He didn't need his mother's money. He worked as a mechanic at a local gas station and was good at his job. But he couldn't remember when he had last bought food. Lately, he hadn't been feeling all that hungry.

There was a black banana in the refrigerator. He almost threw it away, but ended up eating the parts that looked serviceable. Then he found a box of crackers in a cupboard. He was munching on those with the help of a glass of water when he noticed the message light blinking on the answering machine.

His dad had bought the machine for business reasons. It was the newest thing in the house, and one of the most expensive—it cost a hundred bucks. Carl rewound the tape and lowered the volume. The messages his dad's pals left usually contained a minimum of ten obscene words.

"Hi, Carl, this is Tracie White. I hope I'm not calling too late. It's ten-fifteen Thursday night. The reason I'm calling—I was wondering if you wanted to be in our group for the scavenger hunt. We're going to have Rick and Paula and myself. We think you could really help us out. Give me a call if you can. My number's five-five-five-nine-three-seven-two. Take care and hope to talk to you soon."

Carl smiled at the message. Tracie was a good kid. He'd had a crush on her when they were freshmen. She was a slender redhead with cute freckles and a smile as sweet as they made them. When they first met at the beginning of high school, he thought they'd become good friends. But they drifted apart, and now seldom talked; he wasn't sure what had happened. He still had a soft spot for her, though. She had an enthusiastic little-girl quality about her that was infectious. At least she used to have that quality. The last few times they'd talked she was kind of quiet. He must not be the only one going through hard times. He definitely had to make time to take her to a movie or dinner—if she'd go with him. He'd heard she'd won a scholarship to a college up north. Express wasn't a town that kept its young people. It was too small and too hot. Soon Tracie would be moving in higher circles than he was accustomed to.

But today was not the day to get together with Tracie. The Paula mentioned in the message was Tracie's best friend, Paula Morrow, and—by unfortunate coincidence—she had also been Joe Travers's girlfriend. Paula hadn't been keen on Carl since Joe died. He avoided her whenever possible. He wasn't sure, but suspected Paula blamed him for Joe's death. That was understandable—it had been his idea to go for the trip into the desert. On the other hand, he hadn't exactly dragged Joe along. He guessed everybody needed someone to blame.

Anyway, he couldn't be on Tracie's team when he was on Cessy's. He might have had a crush on Tracie once, but they hadn't come up with a word for the way he felt about Cecilia Stepford. *Love* or *lust* didn't say it. He just wanted her, and he wanted her bad.

Tracie must have called after he had gone to bed last night. He decided not to call her back. He'd see her at school and tell her he was already taken. He put away his crackers and went outside and climbed in his truck.

Express was a nothing town. It had roads and buildings and a population of twenty thousand, but when Carl drove around it, he was reminded of the millions of cities listed on a map of the U.S.—all those meaningless names and places that just turned to a gray blur if you held the map out a couple of feet. It didn't make any difference that he'd lived in Express all his life, it wasn't home to him. Sometimes he wondered if he'd ever find any place that felt like home.

Express was located eighty miles inland from San Diego, forty miles north of the Mexican border. Besides the scorching heat, Express had smog. God only knew where it came from. May through September, the town and its people hardly moved.

Mr. Partridge's club members must have strained their imaginations planning the promised scavenger hunt through the all-but-deserted streets of Express. Carl could see them searching for Life Savers in the Rexall Drugs and three-quarter-inch screws in Headly's Hardware. More than that he couldn't imagine. He wasn't even sure what the grand prize was supposed to be.

Cessy lived in an area of town referred to as the Mountains, a creative name for a portion of Express where the ground sloped upward a hundred feet and a herd of eucalyptus trees had gathered. It was where the well-to-do resided. On the way there, thinking of Cessy swimming naked in her pool and nudging his truck toward a red light that didn't have the good sense to turn green, Carl almost ran over Paula Morrow's younger brother, the esteemed Richard Morrow.

"Hey!" Rick shouted, bringing his wheelchair to an abrupt halt three feet short of the projected path of Carl's truck. Carl wouldn't really have hit him. Rick was overreacting, which Carl supposed was his right since he was only fifteen and about to graduate three years early and at the head of *their* class. Carl put his truck in neutral and pulled on the parking brake. Except for the two of them, the intersection was empty. Rick wheeled over to Carl's window. He was breathing heavily. He had muscular dystrophy and had been crippled since age five.

"Were you going to run that light?" Rick asked.

"Probably."

"You didn't see me, did you?"

"Nope. You were moving too fast." Rick put in his road work every morning. One day he said he was going to wheel his chair in the New York Marathon. Carl wished him well, but from the way Rick panted completing his one-mile course every morning, he doubted that Rick would be entering any marathon soon.

Rick grinned at his remark. He was a scrawny kid, with a mop of brown hair that didn't quite hide his big ears. Carl had once heard Tracie call him a choir boy, and that fit. Except for being thin and pale, he looked like a cherub.

"I did a mile on the track the other day and broke five minutes," Rick said. "Ain't bad for a lame duck."

"Were there any witnesses?" Carl asked.

"God was my witness. Hey, did Tracie call you last night?"

Carl hesitated, feeling guilty for not having returned the message. "No," he said.

"She wanted to know if you'd like to be on our team for the scavenger hunt."

"Really?" Carl said.

Rick immediately sensed his lack of interest. He was a sharp kid. "I think we'd make a good team with Tracie's enthusiasm, your brains, and my good looks." He added hastily, "Paula wants you, too."

Carl looked away. He was a lousy liar, except when it came to lying to himself. "Tom said something about my being on his team."

"Tom?" Rick asked.

"Tom Barrett. You know, my friend?" It disturbed him how people had forgotten about Tom now that his head injury kept him from playing the big athlete. Nobody had forgotten Joe—all the touchdowns he had scored. Not that Joe didn't deserve to be remembered.

"Oh, yeah, him," Rick said. "Who else is going to be in the group? If it's just the two of you, maybe we could team up with you?"

"I don't know." Carl raised his head, seeing Rick's eager face. He didn't understand why the kid looked up to him the way he did when Rick's IQ must have been twice his. "Let's see when we all get to school, all right? I might not even take part."

"You got work to do?"

Rick was giving him a polite out. "Yeah," Carl said. "Got a ring job on a semi whose engine melted when it crossed our city line."

Rick wiped the sweat off his brow with the back of his hand. "I believe it. It's supposed to be a hundred and ten today. I hope the scavenger hunt leads us to water."

Carl shivered at the remark, even though the sun beating down on the back of his head was making him feel as if he were a matchstick the sky was trying to light. It made no sense that the dam in his dream should have spouted bloody water. Joe hadn't bled a drop.

"So do I," Carl said without enthusiasm.

Rick said goodbye and continued with his workout. Carl put his truck in gear and ran the light, which had turned green and then red again while they had talked.

Cessy's place was big for Express, and distinctive. The lot had a good percentage of the Mountains' trees, and as Carl drove up the long driveway and into the blessed shade, his spirits began to lift. He had never been inside the brown frame house, but he had been around back once with Tom. Cessy's pool was like an underground lake; huge, with a black bottom—and maybe a white bottom now, too, if Cessy was still swimming nude. He parked and walked around the side of the house without ringing the front doorbell. Cessy's parents were never home.

Cessy was laughing and Tom was spacing when Carl entered the backyard. Surprisingly, Tom caught his attention first. Tom was sitting cross-legged on the white deck at the shallow end. The way the light blazed across the front of Tom's black shirt, Carl figured he must be planted directly in the hottest part of the sun's reflection. Not only that, he didn't have on dark glasses, and he was staring into the very spot where the harshest angle of the sun hit the surface of the pool. He wasn't even squinting.

Tom's eyes weren't following Cessy, either, which might have been a sign of brain damage, but Carl had no such problem. Cessy was at the far end of the pool, in deep water, and with the black bottom it was difficult to tell if she was wearing a suit or not. The uncertainty raised Carl's substantial pulse several extra beats. He strolled toward the deck, trying to look casual. It was a wonderful thing, he thought, when nature placed a wild girl inside the body of a mature woman.

"Hello, kids," he said nonchalantly.

"Hello," Tom said, barely moving an eyebrow. Tom had a wide blunt face, and even under the best of circumstances showed scant emotion. Today didn't look as if it would be one of his better days. A couple of months ago Carl had seen an adaptation of Ray Bradbury's *The Martian Chronicles* on TV, and the bronze masks the Martians wore reminded him of Tom's masklike face. And that saddened him. Before his football accident, Tom had been full of life.

"Hi, Carl," Cessy called, her black curly hair plastered wet and dripping over her eyes. She brushed it aside and grinned at him with her wide mouth. "Want to get wet?"

Carl briefly wondered if he wasn't still at home and dreaming. Cessy was treading water not far from the diving board, and he had been wrong about her *white* bottom. She was definitely naked, he realized, and he could glimpse no break in the uniformity of her

23

wonderful tan. She probably went skinny-dipping all the time. He wished she wouldn't splash quite so much so the water could calm down and let him see . . .

I'm turning into a pervert.

"I didn't bring my suit," he said and blushed in spite of his resolve to be totally cool. Cessy twisted her head toward Tom.

"He doesn't have his suit," she called. "What should we do?"

"I don't know," Tom said.

Cessy knew. "If you can't join me, I suppose I better get out," she remarked, swimming toward Carl. When she reached the side, she held up her arm for a helping hand. The top of her right breast lifted above the water line, and a very fine top of the breast it was. Cessy was built. But not only did she have him distracted, she had him suckered. He had no sooner clasped her wet palm when he was falling head-first into the water.

"Oh, Carl, you're such a doll to join me," Cessy said when he surfaced. She didn't give him a chance to get angry. Splashing him in the face, she darted toward the shallow end with a flirtatious wink that said he was welcome to follow. And follow her he did, with his soaked pants and waterlogged sneakers taking the bite out of his strokes. Or was he just using the clothes as an excuse for not catching her? He was no slouch in the water, but she was an incredible swimmer. Before he could get to the step area, she had flipped over and pushed off the side and passed him underwater like a mermaid riding a torpedo.

"Having fun?" Tom asked.

Carl paused to take a breath. "What time is it?"

Tom consulted his watch. "Late."

Carl tugged at his wet shirt. "I think I'm going to be extra late."

"You can wear my clothes. I've got my gym shorts on underneath these pants. I was going to go swimming in them."

"You sure?"

Tom shrugged. "I don't care what I wear to school."

"Oh, boys," Cessy called. "What time is it?"

Carl received one of the major disappointments of his life when he turned around. Cessy had already climbed out of the pool and was in her bathrobe. He couldn't believe his bad timing, nor could he believe not a flicker of interest had touched Tom's expression, when Tom must have seen the entire transition from water to bathrobe.

"It's late," Carl called, climbing slowly up the pool steps.

It got later before they left for school. Cessy hadn't had breakfast yet, and she swore she just had to have breakfast. She disappeared inside for several minutes, and when she returned—effortlessly balancing a huge red tray in one hand—she had a meal fit for a king and a queen: crisp bacon, fat sausage, scrambled eggs, toast, juice, and a bowl of plump fruit. By this time Carl had changed into Tom's shirt and pants; Tom had even lent him his sandals, preferring, he said, to go barefoot. Cessy still had her white bathrobe on, though, and Carl was thankful for small favors. Her long black hair had already begun to dry into its natural curls. The three of them sat to eat at a round glass table beneath the slanted wooden beams of the porch.

"We're going to miss the assembly on the scavenger hunt," Carl said, trying the bacon and liking it. Cessy must have had the food already prepared before going into the pool, or else there was someone else home. "It's taking the place of first period."

"Davey won't let it start until we get there," Cessy said, munching on two sausages while simultaneously sampling her eggs.

Davey was Cessy's brother. He was senior class president. They were in the same grade. Although the two had only arrived in Express at the end of last summer, and next to no one knew them when school had begun in the fall, Davey had somehow managed to win the office by his extravagant promises. Davey had actually told the class he was going to see to it that they had live entertainment every day at lunch. No one had believed him, but they had voted for him, anyway. He was a smooth talker.

They didn't have live entertainment once the entire year.

"Does Davey know how Mr. Partridge's club has organized the hunt?" Carl asked.

"He says no," Cessy said.

"Do you believe him?" Carl asked.

"He's my brother," she said. "Of course not."

"I'm glad he's on our team then," Carl said. "Maybe we'll win."

Cessy grinned, showing her dimples. Her face was

round, too cute to be called classically beautiful and too sensual to be thought of as innocent. Her lush lips were the first thing a guy noticed about her, if not her wonderful hair. In fantasies, whenever Carl kissed her, he always felt as if he were being eaten alive by those full lips. She swallowed the remains of her sausage and batted her thick black lashes over her dark-blue eyes. She was such a tease.

"I'm not positive Davey knows a shortcut to the jackpot," she said and touched his hand with her fingertip. "That's why we want you on our team. To make sure we win."

"If you're worried about winning," Carl said, pleased with her comment, "then you should have recruited Rick Morrow. He's got the brains."

Cessy glanced at Tom, who was carefully buttering his fourth piece of toast. Any day now he would begin to eat the bread. God only knew how he and vivacious Cessy had become such good friends. "Could we get Master Richard?" she asked.

"He's going to be on a team with his sister and Tracie White," Tom said.

"Who told you that?" Carl asked, curious how Tom had come across the obscure information when he had trouble keeping track of when tomorrow was. But that was the thing about Tom—he was out there in right field with the mushrooms, but he had brought along binoculars and could tell you who was sitting behind the home plate umpire.

"I don't know," Tom said.

"Maybe we could team up with their team halfway through the hunt," Cessy suggested.

Tom paused and put down his butter knife and looked at her. "I heard that's against the rules."

"The rules," Cessy snorted. "Who made those up? Mr. Partridge? That guy's weird. He hasn't taken off his sunglasses once the entire year. You know what I think? I think he's a vampire. He's so pale and gross-looking."

"A friend of mine is in one of his classes," Carl said. "English literature. All he does is have them read books and write reports he never grades. He never lectures."

"I still don't think we need Rick on our team," Tom said.

Cessy returned his look, and had a sudden change of heart. "You're probably right."

"The four of us will be enough," Tom said.

Cessy removed her finger from Carl's hand and reached for the strawberries. "Carl?" she asked. "Did you used to go out with Tracie White?"

"No. Who told you that?"

"No one." Cessy popped a couple of strawberries in her mouth. "It's just the way she looks at you sometimes."

Carl knew Cessy was pulling his leg. "I'm afraid she hasn't had the pleasure," he said, once again trying to sound casual. Light banter didn't come easily for him, especially with a girl as pretty as Cessy. He was much more comfortable crunched on his back beneath an oily engine, even though he hated his job, or at least the joint where he worked. The garage was full of savages. He had to get out of there, and out of Express, too.

Cessy chewed her strawberries slowly, savoring, so it seemed to him, the feel of them in her mouth more than their taste, her wet, white bathrobe almost loose enough to make his disappointment of a few minutes ago a thing of the distant past. She didn't elaborate upon her remark.

"Why do you ask?" he asked finally.

"No reason," she said, and she smiled at him.

CHAPTER

II

*T*RACIE WHITE FELT AS IF SHE WERE RUNNING OUT OF time. Next Friday was the last day of school, and after that she would have no excuse to get together with Carl Timmons. No good excuse. Of course, she could always call him up during the summer and ask him out, but just the thought of it made her stomach queasy. It had taken her an hour of talking to herself to call him the previous night and invite him to join their group. And then he hadn't been there, and she'd had to leave a message. She was a bit surprised, and a little hurt, that he hadn't called her back.

Tracie thought she might be in love with Carl. Her infatuation with him had been going on too long to be labeled a simple crush. She could remember when she met him the first week of their freshman year. She had an art class, and the teacher sent her to fetch a bag of clay from the supply room. Only the bag turned out to be an eighty-pound sack, and she was having a devil of a time getting it back to the class. At eighteen and about to graduate, she was still underweight, but at fourteen and just starting high school, she had been a twig. Fortunately for her and the clay, Carl just happened to walk by.

Tracie didn't believe in love at first sight. It was illogical. How could you love someone you didn't know? Liking the way a guy looked, even lusting after him—sure, that made sense. But to fall in love with someone in the space of three minutes, that was dumb. Yet by the time Carl walked her back to her class, with the sack of clay slung carelessly over one broad shoulder, she was a goner.

To this day Tracie did not understand what had happened in those few minutes. Carl was cute, but her feelings for him had not blinded her into imagining he was a knockout. He had an excellent build and a gorgeous head of blond hair. But there was nothing distinctive about the shape of his face or the color of his eyes. Not if the features were studied from afar, or from, say, a photo. It was only the quiet warmth of his presence that made his brown eyes seem to sparkle, the calm strength of his personality that gave the angles of his mouth and jaw a power that perhaps they did not really possess. Yet it was none of these things that made her love him. She loved him simply because he was Carl.

It all began in minutes, but it might just as well have ended then, too. As the days passed, they became good friends. He would talk with her at lunch, and several times they met after school at the library to study together. They even went for ice cream one Saturday evening when they bumped into each other coming out of the same movie. But as the days turned to months, and the whole of their freshman year and the beginning of their sophomore year, and he never asked her out on a real date, she found talking to him at lunch less satisfying. Painful in a way. The truth hurt. He liked her, obviously, but that was all.

She took to avoiding him. What could she do? And the worst thing was that he didn't even notice that she was doing it. He never stopped her at school to ask her what the problem was. He just went his way, and she went hers and life went on. Nevertheless, she continued to watch him, secretly, waiting for the day he would begin to date someone else. He never did, though, and it made her wonder if maybe she did stand a chance. Near the end of school their junior year, she contemplated calling him, making up some silly excuse why they should get together. She practically had the phone in her hand when his best friend, Joe Travers, died in the desert.

Then *her* best friend, Paula Morrow, told her to stay away from Carl. Paula said he was too bummed out, too angry at the world to talk to anybody. And it was true that when school started the following fall, Carl could often be seen standing by himself. But Paula didn't fool Tracie for a minute. Paula had loved Joe, and now she hated Carl for having survived the desert flood when her boyfriend had not. The animosity went unexpressed, hanging in the air between them like a dark cloud. Occasionally, Tracie wondered whether Paula would remain her friend if she did go out with Carl.

Yet that had all changed a week ago, when out of the blue Paula said they should ask Carl to be in their small group for the scavenger hunt. It was Paula who had given her the courage to call Carl the previous night. Paula's explanation was simple, and uncharacteristically altruistic: her past problems, she said, shouldn't interfere with her friend's future happiness. Besides, her younger brother, Rick, adored Carl and wanted him on their team.

Now Rick was giving Tracie the bad news.

Carl had rejected their offer.

The two of them were waiting outside in the shade of the gym for Paula to show up and the assembly to begin. That was the official reason for their meeting place. In reality, Tracie was waiting for Carl to walk by so she could accidentally bump into him.

And beg him to give me a chance.

"What exactly did he say when you asked him?" Tracie asked.

"I told you," Rick said.

"Tell me again. Word for word."

"First I asked if you called him last night, and he said no."

"But I did call him. I left a message."

"What time?" Rick asked.

"Ten-fifteen."

"That was late."

"You told me he gets off work at nine-thirty."

"But he usually goes straight home and goes to bed," Rick said. "You should have called him at ten."

"Why does he go to bed so early?"

"Beats me, he must be tired. Anyway, then I asked if he wanted to be on our team, and he said his friend Tom had already asked him to be on *his* team."

"Tom who?" Tracie asked.

"Tom Barrett."

"Oh, yeah, that guy. But then you said maybe he and Tom wouldn't mind teaming up with us?"

"No. *I* suggested the two of them team up with us."

"What did he say to that?" Tracie asked.

"That he would have to see when he got to school."

"That sounds OK. Why are you saying he's not interested?"

Before Rick could answer, he suddenly stopped and grimaced. His back arched and his breathing changed to a rapid pant. Tracie did not panic. He often suffered painful back spasms. She automatically reached out to steady his wheelchair. Rick should have given up on the chair a long time ago. His condition was degenerating. He needed motorized wheels. Contrary to the strong image he projected, he was quite weak— weaker than he had been the previous year. She watched with a lump in her throat as he forced himself to bend forward and stretch his muscles against the cramp.

"Are you all right?" she asked.

"Yes."

"Would you like me to massage your back?"

"No. Thank you, I'm fine. Really."

It was not unusual for her to rub his back when they were alone together. She had the greatest hands in the world, he said, and she thought she did have a good touch. Growing up with two younger sisters, she had always been the one to play doctor for whomever was ill. She planned on going to medical school when she graduated from college, even though she had a hard time seeing people in pain.

Rick sat up and took a deep breath, letting it out slowly. The spasm began to subside.

"It wasn't so much what Carl said, but the way he said it," Rick explained, looking up at her. He knew her feelings for Carl. "I'm sorry."

She felt ridiculous having him console her when he was only fifteen and had to struggle an hour every morning just to get out of bed. She leaned over and gave him a hug, burying his pale face in her long red hair.

"What do I need Carl for when you've already promised to marry me?" she said.

"It's a well-known fact nuclear physicists make better lovers than auto mechanics," he agreed, giving her a feeble hug in return.

David Stepford came along shortly thereafter. Next to Carl, Tracie thought he was the most fascinating guy in the school. He had his sister's great looks: big dark-blue eyes, a wide, full-lipped mouth, curly black hair. Indeed, they looked so much alike, Tracie had assumed they were twins. But Davey said they weren't. Then again, his personality differed markedly from Cessy. She was only interested in having fun, but Davey was always maneuvering to get ahead. Tracie admired ambition. She had worked hard to get her scholarship to the University of Berkeley. She waved to Davey and he floated over in his tight white slacks and half-buttoned red shirt.

"Hey, babe," he said, offering his cheek for a kiss. "How come you haven't called recently for the best I can give you?"

She obliged him with a quick peck, saying, "It's hard for a poor working girl such as myself to dream of calling on someone of your high social standing."

"Hey," Rick said. "I hear they're only giving us fifteen minutes each at the graduation ceremony?"

As senior class president, Davey was naturally slated to speak at the ceremony to be held the following Friday. But even though Rick had the only perfect grade point average in the school, he was not valedictorian. The faculty felt he should be considered separately since he had been allowed to skip so many classes. On graduation day, they were giving him a special award and had asked him to speak on technology, pollution, and the responsibilities of their generation to the future, which thrilled him to no end.

"That's true," Davey replied. "But I speak before you, and I'll probably go over a quarter of an hour."

"In that case," Rick said, "I'll change my topic to the problem of noise pollution."

Davey stared at him for a moment before responding and Tracie wondered if Rick had accidentally offended him. But suddenly Davey flashed the dazzling smile that had helped get him elected and slapped Rick on the back.

"You talk about the end of the world if you want, Dick," he said.

Rick smiled. "Rick."

"I'll remember," Davey said.

"There's a rumor going around that you know all the ins and outs of the scavenger hunt," Tracie said.

Davey shook his head. "Cessy started the rumor. It's not true. Only the members of Mr. Partridge's club have the inside scoop, and they're not talking. But I do know something." He leaned closer and spoke confidentially. "Even the club members don't know where the hunt is going to end. Only Mr. Partridge knows."

Tracie had scarcely seen Mr. Partridge the whole year, but Paula had a class with him. She said he was unquestionably the most boring man alive on the planet today.

"But a scavenger hunt is where you go out and collect stuff," Rick said. "Couldn't different groups end up in different places, as long as they've gathered what they were supposed to?"

"It's my understanding that certain articles on the list will be one-of-a-kind items," Davey said.

"You do have inside information," Tracie said.

Davey glanced over his shoulder at a man moving toward the gymnasium. Wearing his usual dark sunglasses and lumbering along as if his long legs were stilts made of petrified wood, Mr. Partridge was heading for the entrance.

"I've heard enough to know it's going to be an interesting day," Davey said, taking a step away. "Excuse me, please."

" 'Bye," Tracie called.

"It's a well-known fact most suave political types are impotent," Rick muttered.

"Jealous?" Tracie asked.

Rick smiled softly. "Yes."

Carl appeared approximately ten minutes later. By then the bulk of the traffic heading into the gym had cleared. The orientation was about to begin. Tracie felt a stab in her gut when she saw Carl. He was with Tom Barrett and Cecilia Stepford. *Cessy!* Tracie wasn't aware that he was interested in her. The two of them were walking close together, laughing easily. Tracie hadn't seen Carl laugh all year.

"Is it a well-known fact that guys like girls with bodies like hers?" she asked Rick.

"I haven't seen any research on the subject."

"I have," she said flatly.

"You're the last person I thought I'd see give up without a fight." Rick reached over and squeezed her hand. "Go get him. I'll meet you inside."

"All right." As Rick wheeled away, Tracie tried to prepare herself mentally. People saw her as a spunky go-getter, and usually she was, except when it came to trying to get what she *really* wanted. She tentatively raised her arm and waved.

"Hey, Carl!"

He paused midstride when he saw her and stopped laughing. The strange, quiet kid named Tom, wearing nothing but a T-shirt and gym shorts, continued on toward the gym without breaking stride. Cessy giggled and waved back. She grabbed Carl's arm and pulled him in her direction. It was not the way Tracie would have planned it. Cessy had on a loose white dress that might have reached midthigh if only she stood still long enough. Her deeply tanned body was nothing short of sensational.

Ordinarily, Tracie did not suffer from insecurities about her appearance. She had a pretty delicate face, with well-defined cheekbones and a proud chin. Like most redheads, she was fair, and if the summer sun didn't make her burn, it usually gave her another dozen cute freckles. Her only problem was she could not gain weight. She had too much energy and burned too many calories. It didn't matter what she ate—when she turned sideways, her shadow disappeared.

She *would* have disappeared in Cessy's shadow.

"Hi, Tracie," Cessy said, letting go of Carl's arm and standing about a foot closer than was comfortable. "Carl and I were just talking about you at breakfast."

God, did he spend the night with her?

Tracie smiled. "Is that why my ears were burning on the way to school?"

"No, it's why Carl's cheeks were burning," Cessy said, tossing her jumbled head of black curls. It looked like she had gone swimming and forgotten to comb her hair. She still looked great.

Carl shifted uneasily. "I got your message. I was going to call you back."

"That's OK," Tracie said quickly.

"I went to bed early," Carl said.

"It was dumb of me to call so late," Tracie said.

Cessy nodded. "It's better to get him at dawn before he goes for his morning swim." She tapped Tracie on the shoulder. "Why don't you two talk? I have to go listen to Davey's introductory speech and be bored." Cessy poked Carl in the side. "I'll be sitting with Tom if you need to find me."

They watched her leave. Like her brother, she moved gracefully. Only Cessy bounced more than Davey did. "She's so friendly," Tracie remarked.

"She's a nice girl," Carl agreed. He raised his arm to wipe the sweat off his forehead with the back of his sleeve, then changed his mind. The black shirt looked a size too small for him. The strong muscles of his chest pressed against the material. "The orientation is going to start any minute," he said.

"You're right. We should get inside."

"Yeah," he said. But neither made a move to leave. Carl studied the sky and Tracie looked at the ground. Just a couple years ago they had been able to talk for hours and never run out of things to say. "How have you been?" he asked finally.

"Great. I'm going to Berkeley in the fall."

"I heard you won a scholarship."

"Yeah. It pays for my tuition, but I'll still have to work part-time to cover room and board. I don't mind, though." She gestured to the blazing sun. "Anything to get out of this oven."

"I hear you. Well, that's great. I'm happy for you."

"What have you been up to? I haven't talked to you much lately."

He shrugged. "When I'm not here, I'm working."

"What station is that again?"

"Trask's, on Canyon Ave."

"I drive by there all the time." She hesitated. "I should stop in and see you sometime."

"I wouldn't bother," he said. "The place is a dump."

"Oh. OK." She felt a knot forming in her chest. He wasn't even interested in her as a friend anymore. She should stop now before she made a complete fool of herself.

Yet she thought of how long the summer was going to be sitting beside a phone she knew wasn't going to ring.

"The reason I called last night," she began, knowing he already knew the reason. "I was wondering if you wanted to be on our team for the scavenger hunt? It would be Rick, Paula, and me. And Paula says she'd really like to have you and everything." She smiled. "I think the four of us working together could win the grand prize."

"What is the grand prize?"

She forced a laugh. "Beats me."

Carl regarded her closely. He had lost weight since last year, and he looked tired. She wondered if he still missed Joe, but of course he must. Joe had been one hell of a guy, as easygoing as they came, someone who never gave a thought for himself. Tracie still had trouble convincing herself he was gone. He had been a big part of her life. She had seen him all the time at Paula's house.

"I'm sorry," Carl said. "Tom has asked me to be on his team. I already said I would."

"Is it just the two of you? You could team up with us."

"No. There're already four of us."

"Oh. Who else?" Dumb question.

"Cessy and Davey."

She smiled, dying inside, and furious with herself that she should feel so much over so little. She would see him all next week. She would probably bump into him throughout the day on the scavenger hunt. There was plenty of time to set up something with him before he disappeared forever.

Into Cessy's arms.

"Sounds like an interesting combination," she said.

"I better get inside," he said.

She nodded. "Goodbye."

Paula had been waiting in the gym the whole time. Tracie found her and Rick on the bottom bleacher against the far wall. Paula only needed one more week and she would have her diploma. Yet she was risking expulsion by smoking a cigarette in full view of half the faculty.

Paula had gone wild since she had lost her boyfriend. She hung out with Jacob High's worst—a loose group of two dozen guys and girls who would have been called bikers had many of them been able to afford motorcycles and leather jackets. They drank beer more often than smoked pot, and did not accost Express's innocent bystanders. On the other hand, most of them were still in high school, and Tracie thought it was only a matter of time before they all ended up behind bars. She had the horrible fear that she would get a call one night from the police telling her that Paula needed to raise bail, or worse, that she had been involved in a confrontation with officers, and that she was at the hospital.

Paula's appearance had altered to match that of her new friends. She used to have long, wavy blond hair, but recently had cut it short. She either wore gobs of purple eye shadow and tons of cheap jewelry with pink halter tops, or else wore no makeup and a torn Levi jacket. She chain-smoked, and stank of smoke. Her favorite word was *goddamn*.

The pattern was not complex. Paula had lost her love and now she was angry at the world. Yet she hadn't gone downhill immediately after Joe's death. It had only been months later, toward the end of summer, when the authorities found his body buried beneath a pile of dried earth that the bad days had begun. She fainted when they'd lowered Joe's coffin into the ground, and had woken up swearing instead of crying. If it hadn't been for her younger brother, Paula would have chucked school altogether and taken off for L.A., Tracie thought.

Paula didn't baby Rick. She was harder on him than anybody. If they were eating at McDonald's and he needed catsup for his fries, she made him get it, even though the condiments were on top of a high shelf. Rick had to undo his belt and lasso the tiny plastic pouches. Paula seldom helped him get out of the car the few mornings their drunkard mother got up the energy to drive them to school.

But all this was to make Rick self-sufficient, and only Tracie knew how much it hurt Paula not to help him. Not even Rick knew, although he was fiercely devoted to his sister. She was the only one who was always there for him when he really needed someone. Their dad was worse than their mom, usually off gambling and fooling around south of the border. Tracie wouldn't be surprised if neither parent came to the graduation ceremony to watch Rick receive his award and listen to his speech.

"Put out that cigarette," Tracie said, sitting down beside Paula and behind Rick's wheelchair.

"When I'm done," Paula said, taking a drag. Tracie reached over and snapped it from her fingers and ground it out beneath her white tennis shoes.

"They give you bad breath," Tracie said.

"Here, here," Rick said.

Paula was not put out. She smoked to make a statement, not because she enjoyed it. She pulled a stick of gum from her tight jean pockets and popped it in her mouth. She liked gum. "Where were you guys?" she growled.

"Waiting for Carl to come by," Tracie said. "He doesn't want to be on our team."

"A pity," Paula said.

"I'm sure you're disappointed," Tracie said.

Paula looked over at her. "I'm sorry."

"Yeah."

"I *am* sorry. Look, I'm the one who told you to call him." She paused. "Why doesn't he want to be on our team? Aren't we good enough for him?"

"Cessy's asked him to be on her team," Tracie said.

"I thought it was Tom who asked him," Rick said.

"Who's Tom?" Paula said.

"Cessy and Davey are going to be on his team as well," Tracie explained to Rick, before turning back to Paula. "Tom Barrett, Carl's friend."

"Oh, him." Paula made a face. "That guy gives me the creeps."

"Why?" Tracie asked.

"I don't know, just something about him," Paula said, distracted. "So are you going to kill yourself or do you give a damn?"

"You might want to offer her a third choice," Rick suggested.

"I'm disappointed," Tracie said.

Paula twisted her head to the right, scanning the crowd. "Are the four of them sitting together?"

"I don't know," Tracie said. "I don't want to know."

"Tom Barrett," Paula muttered to herself, puzzled. "Are you sure that's his last name?"

"It's Barrett," Rick said confidently.

"What is it?" Tracie asked Paula.

"Nothing."

The orientation started then. The crowd was three hundred strong—Jacob High's entire senior class. They settled into an expectant silence as Davey stepped to the microphone. Talk about the scavenger hunt had been circulating for over a month. There was nothing like a total lack of available information on a subject to heighten interest in it. All that was really known about the hunt was that the grand prize was supposed to be incredible.

Davey did not give the boring speech Cessy feared. He simply welcomed everyone, introduced Mr. Partridge and returned to his seat. Mr. Partridge stood slowly and made his way toward the microphone. It took him awhile to cover the distance. The man looked ill. His limbs were glued together at the joints. If he didn't have arthritis, he should have had it; whatever he did have was worse. Also, had he been a pound thinner, his clothes would have slipped off him onto the floor, which might have been a blessing in disguise. He was dressed weird. Ordinarily, he wore boring black slacks and white starched shirts with bright red bowties. Today he had on hiking clothes, every item of which was charcoal gray. The effect was as if he had been outfitted, and then stepped in front of a chimney sweep, who was cleaning his brushes.

Then there were his sunglasses. They were silver— like mirrors. He never took them off. He had explained to Paula's English lit class that he'd caught a virus in the Orient years ago that had made him permanently sensitive to bright light. Despite being a bore, however, he was supposed to be friendly.

"Hello," he said in his slow, dry voice. "We'll need everybody sitting in his or her team before we can begin. Remember, four is the ideal number, but you may have one less or one more if you must." He nodded to a group of kids sitting up front. "Hand out the materials as soon as everybody is properly arranged." He then added for the benefit of the audience as a whole, "Read the contents as soon as you receive the envelopes."

The reorganization took only a minute. They had been warned the previous day to sit in teams. The kids in Mr. Partridge's club went through the crowd with their manila envelopes, giving one to each team. Rick accepted their copy from Davey, who was helping with the distribution. Rick opened it and pulled out a single sheet of paper. Paula and Tracie peered over his shoulder as the three of them read it together.

Scavenger Hunt

1. The beginning and the end of a dirt path that goes on forever, where the water flows hidden beneath blades of green
2. A tall tree
3. A place on a course
4. The finest selection
5. At the best prices
6. A metal grave
7. Two of a kind
8. All alone with nothing around

9. Wrong turn
10. A place without a beginning, without an end, where the waters flow hidden beneath an empty sky

"What the hell is this?" Paula asked.

"It looks neat," Rick said, excited.

"What's the answer?" Tracie asked, half expecting him to have already figured it out.

"I'm sure we'll be given more instructions," Rick said. "But I can see already that this isn't going to be your ordinary scavenger hunt."

"How so?" Tracie asked.

"This is some kind of map," Rick said.

Mr. Partridge did indeed have a few things left to explain. When he was satisfied everybody had reviewed the sheet, and after exchanging a quick word with Davey, he returned to his spot behind the microphone.

"What you have in front of you is a list of clues that have been designed to lead you to ten different places," Mr. Partridge said. "Except for the first one, the clues are incomplete. Don't even try to figure them out now. When you get to point one, you'll find the other half of clue two, and only then will it make sense. When you reach point two, you'll find the other half of clue three, and so on. You cannot reach the second location without going to the first, and you cannot reach the third location without going to the second. Is this clear? Raise your hand if it is not."

There were no questions. Mr. Partridge continued, "You will find something else at each location—the items you must collect in order to win the scavenger hunt. There will be more than one of each item at each place, but there will not be enough for every team. For that reason, the item will be clearly listed at each location. If you get there late, you will have to try to find it elsewhere. But you will know what it is you have to find. You can either get it at home or purchase it if you wish. Is this clear?"

Again, there were no questions. The crowd was dead silent. Either they were exceptionally attentive or else Mr. Partridge's monotone voice was putting them to sleep. He cleared his raspy throat and went on.

"While on the hunt, there are a number of rules you must follow. First, you cannot go outside your own team for assistance, either to solve a clue or to obtain one of the items. Second, you cannot take more than one of the items from each location, or in any way damage the clues or items listed there. If a team breaks any of these rules, they will be immediately disqualified. Members of my club will be supervising each locale. Even if you don't see them, know that they are around. By the way, there is no time limit to this hunt. It can go on all day and all night, and lead you to where you least expect. When you reach the final location, you will know what to do with the items you have collected."

For the third time he asked if there were any questions. There was only one, and half a dozen kids called it out simultaneously.

What was the grand prize?

"A one-week all-expense-paid vacation to Hawaii for each member of the winning team," Mr. Partridge said.

The crowd gasped. Then they began to cheer. A few shouted questions about any runner-up prizes. Mr. Partridge adjusted his sunglasses and flashed a rare smile.

"There is only going to be one winner." He raised a stiff arm and waved. "Good luck, everybody. You may begin now. Happy hunting."

CHAPTER
III

CESSY DRAGGED TOM AND CARL OUTSIDE THE INSTANT
Mr. Partridge gave his go-ahead. She was excited.
"What does this first clue mean?" she kept asking.

Carl laughed. He couldn't get over his good fortune
at being on Cessy's team. She genuinely seemed to like
him. Asking her out when they were finished for the
day, he thought, should be no snap. And imagine if
they won, and were able to go to Hawaii together? The
thought of it made his head whirl. On the islands
they'd have the whole Pacific Ocean to go skinny-
dipping in.

Yet he kept his good feelings on a leash, afraid to let
them run away with him and leave him empty-
handed. He was not the first guy Cessy had flirted with
this school year, and even though there was only a
week left of class, he probably wouldn't be the last.

"Shouldn't we wait for Davey?" Carl asked.

"Here I am," Davey called, making his way out the
jammed side door. They had avoided the stampede by
seconds. Wouldn't it be ironic if the first clue referred
to a place inside the gym? Davey disentangled himself

smoothly from the crowd and offered Carl his hand. "I'm glad you could join us," he said.

"I appreciate you having me," Carl said.

"The beginning and the end of a dirt path that goes on forever," Cessy said, reading from the paper in her hands. "Where the water flows hidden beneath blades of green." She turned impatiently to her brother. "Just tell us, Davey. At least the first one, so we can get started."

Davey was annoyed. "Would you stop that. You have half the school distrusting me. I have to figure these things out just like everybody else."

Cessy stared at him for a moment before smiling. "All right, brother, I believe you." She turned to Tom. "Any ideas?"

"Blades of green probably means grass," Tom said.

"That's right," Carl said, impressed.

"But where does water flow hidden beneath the grass around here?" Cessy asked.

"Lots of places," Davey said. "There're pipes under most of the school."

"Does it have to be in the school?" Carl asked.

"From what Mr. Partridge explained, I would say no," Davey said. "Let's look at that part about a dirt path that goes on forever. It sounds like a metaphor."

Carl nodded, thoughtful. "A metaphor for a circle. But where do we have a circular dirt path that—" He clapped his hands together. "The track!"

"Not so loud," Cessy cautioned, glancing over her shoulder.

"But isn't the track oval-shaped?" Tom asked.

"It doesn't matter," Carl said. "It still goes on forever."

Davey's face brightened. He slapped Carl on the back. "I think we're on our way to Hawaii."

They followed the ramp behind the gym up to the stadium. There was already a team on the track at the post where the races usually started and ended: Tracie, Rick, and Paula. Rick had probably deciphered the clue before Mr. Partridge finished talking. They hurried over to Tracie's team. Paula was pulling up a drain cover beside the starting post.

"We should have known it would be you guys," Davey said. "Is there anything there?"

"We can't tell you," Rick said. "But you can look for yourself."

They gathered around the underground space where the overflow from the sprinklers drained. There was a cardboard box in it now, instead of water, and it held a dozen identical hunting knives. Tom picked one up.

"This is good quality," he said, slipping it in his belt.

Paula also grabbed a knife and glanced up at him. "Do you collect weapons, dude?" she asked.

Tom did not respond, but merely lowered his head. Cessy got down on her knees in the grass by the hole. "Where's the clue that goes with number two on our paper?" she asked.

It was typed on a piece of paper taped to the side of the box. It said: *That is no longer so.* Beneath it in capital letters were the words: HUNTING KNIFE.

"A tall tree," Rick said, putting the two clues together. "That is no longer so."

"Sounds to me like the stump by the administration building," Davey said. Everyone looked at him in surprise. He laughed and shrugged his shoulders. "It was so obvious. What difference does it make? We can walk there together."

"What if we're being watched?" Rick asked.

"We'll tell them we both figured it out right away," Davey said. "Besides, I think that whole thing about being under surveillance is just a scare tactic."

Davey could be persuasive, and in a sense they weren't actually breaking the rules. Rick and the girls must have figured out the clue the instant they read it—Carl had. But Carl did not discard the possibility they were being watched through binoculars. He had an uncanny feeling that someone had an eye on them.

Carl was both relieved and disappointed when Tracie and Paula immediately fell behind their team. He didn't understand why he should feel uncomfortable being seen by Tracie with Cessy. Perhaps he was suffering from guilt about having rushed to Cessy's swimming pool when he should have taken a minute to call Tracie. Guilt—sometimes it seemed to him the only emotion holding his insides together. That and regret. He looked back at his life and wondered where he had been while it had taken place. He had gone through the motions for the last four years. He had gone to school, got his driver's license and a job, and he had done nothing. The only times he had felt even remotely alive were when he had gone hiking in the mountains and the desert with Joe, when they had sat together late at night beside a crackling fire, talking about the future. Joe had always been looking forward to what the years would bring. But all they had brought him was what they brought everyone in the end—only a whole lot sooner. Poor Joe.

Carl glanced over his shoulder. He would've liked to have told Tracie again that he was sorry. It wasn't often anyone wanted him for anything. Cessy noticed his glance and touched his shoulder.

"Having fun?" she asked.

"Yes," he said. He supposed he was.

They were at the bottom of the ramp and heading into the shadow of the gym and past the teams that were still stuck on the first clue—which appeared to be *everyone* except them—when Davey brought up an interesting article he'd read in the paper.

"I think it was in Sunday's paper," he said. "San Diego's *Times*. You might find this particularly interesting, Rick. It was about a gold mine in the desert not far from here. They called it Valta."

"Strange name for a mine," Rick said, cocking an ear. He was between Carl and Davey, keeping pace with them.

"The mine had a strange history," Davey said. "It was dug out toward the end of the gold rush days by a group of three men and one woman. The vein turned out to be one of the richest in the state. Working without any outside help, the group took five million dollars' worth of gold out of it. That's five million in eighteen-sixty dollars."

Rick whistled. "They probably could have bought California for that back then."

Davey shook his head. "None of them got to spend a cent of it. The gold was left unclaimed in bank deposit boxes in San Francisco, along with a map describing the location of Valta. Apparently after taking the gold to San Francisco, the group decided to return to search the mine one last time to see if they missed anything. Unfortunately, there was a cave-in or something. They all died."

"Did someone find the map and trace them to Valta?" Rick asked.

"Yes," Davey said. "The president of the bank where they stored the gold. He headed straight to the mine without going to the police. The bank must have had records stating who the money belonged to, but I guess they didn't make any mention of the map. The bank president probably figured he could pick himself up a few nuggets and no one would be the wiser. This was about a year after the others had disappeared. But when he got to the mine, he found the entrance blocked with stone and gravel. He had to labor for over a month to get inside. Then when he did break through, all he found were a couple of skeletons."

"Only two?" Rick asked. "What about the other two?"

"The guy didn't see them," Davey said. "But he figured at first they must have been in there or else the people would've returned for their money. Anyway, the bank president found something else. It was a diary. One of the skeletons was holding it in his bony hands."

"His bony hands?" Rick interrupted, always a stickler for details. "Were both the skeletons male?"

"Interesting you should ask that. The article said they were."

"Go on," Rick said. "What was in the diary?"

Davey smiled. "The paper thought the guy who wrote it must have been delirious from oxygen deprivation. He said that the mine was haunted, and that anybody who entered it should leave immediately before it was too late. He said that all the gold they'd uncovered was worthless."

"Was it fool's gold?" Rick asked.

"Not worthless in that sense. It couldn't have meant that. These people could tell the difference between the real thing and fake. Here's where it gets interesting. The bank president returned to his home in San Francisco. He brought the diary with him, but no gold—he couldn't find any. But as soon as he got back, he was arrested. The gold the others had deposited was gone. Everyone figured the president had stolen it. He was the only one who had the keys to the safety boxes. But he swore he hadn't touched it. He eventually got out on bail. He was a widower. He told his only child, a daughter, about the map and what he'd found in the mine. He gave her the diary. Then he disappeared."

"Where did he go?" Rick asked.

"No one knows for sure. He never came back. But the daughter believed he returned to the mine. It didn't look like he was going to win his trial. She thought he had gone to the mine in the hope he would find enough gold to allow the two of them to flee the country. He never told her what he had planned."

"Maybe he did find gold and split without her," Rick suggested.

"The daughter said he would never have done that. She thought he died in the mine, like the others."

"From another cave-in?" Rick asked.

"Maybe, maybe not," Davey said. "The woman spent years studying the diary. She became convinced that the man who wrote it hadn't been crazy. She thought the mine *was* haunted, and that her father ended up another victim of its evil. That's why she destroyed the diary. She was afraid someone would use it to piece together where the mine was."

"What about the gold in the bank?" Rick asked.

"To this day, no one knows what became of it."

"And the map?"

"The man took it with him when he left for the last time." Davey glanced down at Rick again. "But the daughter did divulge certain points to various people over the years regarding the mine's whereabouts. Taken separately, the information wouldn't have led a person anywhere. But the individual who researched Valta put together enough facts to figure the mine must lie approximately fifty miles east of here, near Rust Valley."

"I know that area," Tom spoke up. "Carl, we've been there, haven't we?"

"Rust Valley?" Carl said, frowning, unable to place it. "Does it have another name?"

"Valta probably has another name," Davey said. "Rick, do you know why I'm telling you all this?"

"You want me to find the mine?" Rick said.

"The kid *is* a genius," Davey said.

Rick nodded. "I'm smart enough to know that half the people who read that article must be thinking of trying to find it."

"Hear me out," Davey said. "Of course I realize that if the mine was easy to locate, it would have been found by now, if by nobody else than the person who researched the subject. But here's where we have an edge over him. We know a local librarian with an unusual passion for local history."

"Mrs. Farley?" Rick asked. Mrs. Farley was the town's head librarian. She was a busy woman, even in a city like Express where the main avenue of intellectual stimulation was provided by cable TV.

"Yes," Davey said. "She has a closet full of documents that go back to when there were only Indians and Spaniards trampling around this neck of the woods. Not once in the article did the author quote her. I don't think he knows about her."

"Chances are she read the article and has already gotten in contact with him," Rick said.

"I doubt she even reads contemporary papers," Davey said. "Look, it's worth a try. Why not talk to her and see if she'll let you dig into her stuff?"

"Why me?" Rick asked. "Why not you?"

"Two reasons," Davey said. "First, Mrs. Farley adores you and hates me, and don't ask me why. She wouldn't let me near her documents. Second, I don't have the patience or the time to search through boxes of old papers for something that the odds are a thousand to one against me finding."

"That's a straight answer," Rick said. He considered a moment. "I guess it wouldn't hurt to give it a try. When was that article printed?"

"Last Sunday, I think, but I can't be sure," Davey said. "Cessy accidentally threw out the paper."

"I threw it out on purpose," Cessy said cheerfully, apparently uninterested in Davey's story. Carl had found it fascinating. When he was young, he loved tales of buried treasure. That was one of the reasons he was enjoying the scavenger hunt. He wondered if

Rust Valley was another name for Red Ravine. He had hiked the ravine several times with Joe.

"One thing," Rick said. "If I find the mine, and it's still got gold in it, how are we going to split the money? It's seems to me I'm going to be doing the majority of the work."

"Yes, but I turned you onto the prospect," Davey said. "We'll split it equally."

"No doubt the original miners made the same agreement," Cessy said.

The stump, located on the north side of the administration building, where pedestrian traffic was sparse, proved to be point two on Mr. Partridge's list. They were off to a flying start. This cardboard box wasn't actually sitting on top of the stump, but under a nearby bush where it would have been hard to miss once the riddle had been solved. Inside were a dozen black-plastic wristwatches. Paula and Tom took one each. Already the two had fallen into the roles of caring for the items. But whereas Tom was sporting his knife in his belt, and was quick to put on the watch, Paula was keeping her things in her pockets. Carl couldn't help noticing how she hadn't looked at him once since they had bumped into each other on the track. He hated when people hated him, especially when he honestly felt no hatred for anyone.

The typed page on the side of the box described the contents for those who arrived too late to get one of the twelve watches. It also contained the clue: *That makes the hardy gasp.*

"Sounds mysterious," Cessy said.

"Maybe our two teams should go our separate ways from now on," Rick said to Davey.

"You've figured it out?" Davey asked.

"No comment," Rick said.

"I'm sure we'll be seeing each other later," Davey said. "Should you stumble across any treasure in the meantime, remember our deal."

"I will," Rick said with a mischievous grin.

CHAPTER
IV

TRACIE AND PAULA WERE IN THE PARK. RICK HAD DI-rected them there. He said *"A place on a course that makes the hardy gasp"* had to be the top of the sole hill on the school's cross-country course. The course was not located on campus, but in the only place in town that could even remotely be referred to as a garden spot. Actually, the park was not that bad. It had swings, four tennis courts, a few trees and an artificial lake. The lake was made more artificial by the pink plastic swans that floated—anchored would have been more accurate—in its center. Last year the city council had allotted funds to bring in a dozen real ducks, only to have the birds fly west toward the ocean at the first heat wave. Smart birds.

Rick was waiting back at the car. His wheelchair wasn't too swift over the grass. Already he was begin-ning to tire.

"Don't you sometimes feel that if God had in-tended for anyone to live here, he'd lower the flame?" Paula asked as the two of them hiked toward the hill.

"I like to think that growing up in Express will make me appreciate wherever it is I end up living," Tracie said.

"You must be looking forward to getting to Berkeley," Paula said.

"Yeah. It's going to be a long summer. I'm working the register and shelving books six days a week at the mall bookstore."

"That joint pays nothing. What do they give you?"

"A quarter an hour above minimum," Tracie said.

"How can you stand it? Why don't you come work with me?"

"Emphysema and brain damage aren't worth another dollar an hour to me." Paula worked in a foam rubber factory. The fumes were incredible. She was there full-time even with school still on—three to twelve Monday through Friday. Many from her "tough crowd" also worked there. They were all going to quit the same day, they said, the day they burned down the place.

Paula snickered. "Is that what's wrong with me?"

"Why don't you come with me?" Tracie asked suddenly.

"To where?"

"Berkeley."

"What are you talking about?" Paula said. "I can't get into college, much less Berkeley."

"You used to devour books. Anyway, you don't have to go to school there. You can just live in the town. We could get a place together. I don't have to stay in the dorm if I don't want to. Rick could come with us. Come on, you must have some money saved."

Paula spit out her gum and reached for a cigarette. "Not a cent."

"Paula! What have you done with your last twenty paychecks?"

"I have expensive habits."

"Don't B.S. me."

"I hand my paychecks over to Harve and he lets me sit on the back of his bike," Paula said, lighting her cigarette and blowing a cloud of smoke into the smoggy sky. Harve was the boy she hung out with now. He was one of the few guys in the gang who had a motorcycle. He had a great body and leather boots and a personality that had about as much going for it as a piece of stale salami. Tracie viewed him as another way for Paula not to have to think about Joe.

"You disgust me," Tracie said. "At least you could think of Rick before saying no. At least *he* could get into Berkeley."

Paula looked in the direction of the lake and the perpetually smiling swans. "I think," she said softly, "the doctors could be even more expensive there."

Tracie stopped dead in her tracks. "What happened to your dad's insurance?"

"It lapsed. That happens when you don't pay the premium."

"You've got to be kidding? Rick's uninsured? You can't afford his doctor bills on what you make."

"You're right there, sister."

"Can you get some other insurance?" Tracie asked.

"They only give health insurance to healthy people."

"How come your parents let it lapse?"

"Because they're uncaring, ignorant bastards," Paula said. "Do you have any other questions?"

"No. I'm sorry."

Paula threw down her cigarette and ground it out in the grass. "So am I." Suddenly, she put a hand to her head, covering her eyes. "Christ."

"Paula," Tracie said, going to put an arm around her. Paula waved her away.

"It's too hot for that crap," she said, taking down her hand. Her cheeks were not damp, but her eyes were red. "He's sick, Tracie. He won't be going to college. He won't be leaving here. So neither will I."

"How sick is sick?"

"I asked the doctor that same question. I was waiting for him to say how Rick could end up incapacitated in a few years. And you know what he told me?"

"No."

Paula chuckled without humor. "He said he could die. Can you believe that?"

"No."

Paula began to speak, then stopped. "I do," she said.

"How long did he give him?"

"A year. Three years. They don't know."

"But muscular dystrophy doesn't have to be fatal. There are many cases where people live full lives."

"I guess this isn't one of those cases."

Tracie was having trouble accepting the news. That was the problem, though. She could see Rick's health was failing, but it was much easier to focus on his strengths than his weaknesses. So what if he missed a couple of days of school a week? He got A's on all his tests.

"Maybe they'll find a cure soon," Tracie said. "Something will come up."

"Joe used to tell me things like that." Paula shook her head. "Nothing will come up. It never does."

They walked the remainder of the distance to the hilltop in silence. It was a steep incline; the runners must have dreaded it. Neither Tracie nor Paula was surprised to see Rick had been right about the spot being point number three on Mr. Partridge's list. The kid was making the two of them feel like spare luggage.

There was no one else around. They had to be in first place. Their spirits lifted when they realized they might all be flying to Hawaii together.

Tracie wished there were four of them going to Hawaii. It had killed her seeing Carl walking with Cessy.

This time the item was a white sock. The box held a dozen of them, and had the words WHITE SOCK printed on the side. There was also the next clue. Unlike the others, it did not read like the second half of a sentence. It said, "That boy is our last hope." "No, there is another."

"Who wrote these things?" Paula complained.

"Those lines sound familiar to me," Tracie said.

"Are you serious?"

"I am."

"How does this go with the line, 'The finest selection'?"

"Give me a few minutes," Tracie said.

Paula stuffed one of the socks in a pocket. "Let's get back to Rick before Mr. Tom and his gang shows."

They started back down the hill. "Why are you giving Tom such a hard time?" Tracie asked. "He seems like a nice guy."

"A hard time? I thought I was flirting with him."

"Right. Sure."

"Honestly." Paula smiled. "He is sort of cute."

The park and the town library shared the same parking lot. Tracie owned a rebuilt red Camaro that she thought was a steal at the time of purchase, but now realized had been a rip-off. She could climb in it at home and drive the two miles to the bookstore where she worked, and the gas gauge would drop a quarter of a tank. The engine was making funny noises. She was afraid to take it into the station and hear the bad news. Of course, if she had the nerve to ask him, Carl would probably fix it for free.

They had left Rick in the front seat of the Camaro beneath a shady tree. The car was still there, but he was gone. They assumed he'd had to use the bathroom in the library. Being crippled, finding a bathroom he could get into and out of was often a major production. He would never let Paula help him onto a toilet.

The temperature dropped a respectable forty degrees the instant they stepped inside the library. Sighing with relief, they both headed straight for the drinking fountain, and when they were through gorging themselves on water, they waited outside the men's restroom for ten minutes. Only Rick didn't show up. Then Tracie remembered the article Davey had been talking about. Although she and Paula had been keeping their distance, she had caught a lot of it.

She'd found the story intriguing. She told Paula they'd probably find Rick in the back searching for a reference to Valta.

Mrs. Farley met them at the front desk and confirmed her hunch. She was a big brunette, on the gray side of forty. There was a persistent rumor going around town that Mrs. Farley had been a professional wrestler, when Tracie knew for a fact she had been a professional roller skater. She loved books, however, and if she saw you reading one, there was a good chance she would love you, too. She was only too happy to lead them to a back corner of the library, where Rick had already buried himself beneath a pile of old papers. Rick was one of Mrs. Farley's prize people.

"He won't even tell me what he's looking for," she said, shaking her head, but looking down upon him fondly. Rick caught their eyes briefly and smiled back up at her.

"It's because I don't know," he said.

"But if it has to do with local history," Mrs. Farley insisted, "you could waste a lot of time searching for something I could direct you to in minutes."

"But if things don't go as I plan," Rick said, "and I'm later arrested, then you could be prosecuted as an accomplice in a crime. The less you know the better."

Mrs. Farley laughed at his remark. Then someone rang the bell at the front desk and she excused herself.

"Why don't you let her help you?" Paula asked, when they were alone.

"You heard what Davey said?" he asked.

"Yes," Paula said. Tracie nodded.

"Well, I haven't been able to find the article he

described," Rick said. "And I've checked all the local papers back a month." He frowned. "I suppose it's possible he read the story in an L.A. paper."

"Let's worry about this later," Paula said. "You were right about the hill on the cross-country course. We've got to keep going. The next clue says—"

"In a moment," Rick interrupted, reaching for a thin parched newspaper. "Let me show you what I did find. This paper is dated June sixth, 1862. It contains an article about Valta. There really was a gold mine by that name. It was located not too far from here. Now I haven't had a chance to read the entire article, but already I can see that some of what Davey said was true, and some was false. For example—"

"Rick," Paula said, plucking the paper from his hand. "We're talking about a trip to Hawaii here. Valta can wait. All right?"

Rick hesitated. "Fine. What was the next item?"

"A white sock," Tracie said.

"One or two?" Rick asked.

"We took only one," Paula said. "It said *a* white sock on the side of the box."

"How many were there in the box?" Rick asked.

"Twelve," Tracie said.

Rick nodded. "Then you probably did the right thing. What's the next clue?"

"Two lines, in quotes," Tracie said, and told him the lines. "What do you think? They sound familiar to me. I remember—" She suddenly stopped. "Yoda!"

"Huh?" Paula said. "That muppet from *Star Wars?*"

"From *The Empire Strikes Back*, the second *Star*

Wars," Tracie said, excited. "When Luke Skywalker left to go fight Darth Vader, Obiwan's ghost said to Yoda, 'That boy is our last hope.'"

"And Yoda said, 'No, there is another,'" Paula finished. "Come on, let's go."

"Yeah," Tracie said.

Rick cleared his throat. "Excuse me. *Where* are we going?"

Tracie and Paula stopped dead in their tracks. "He has a point there," Tracie muttered. "All right, what are we missing?"

"Let's look at how this clue relates to number four," Rick said, pulling the paper out of his shirt pocket. "'The finest selection,'" he quoted, then thought for a moment. "I agree the lines you mentioned must be in reference to the *Star Wars* movie. But since that movie hasn't played in town in many years, the clue must be pointing us to a video cassette of it, or better yet, toward a video store." He paused. "What's the name of that video rental on Bennett Street?"

"Movie Marvels!" Tracie said, bouncing up on her toes. "And they've got this big sign out front that says they've got 'The Finest Selection'!" She leaned over and kissed Rick on the forehead. "You're incredible!"

Rick beamed. "A hug and a kiss in the space of two hours. This must be my lucky day." He gestured to the old paper Paula still had in her hand. "I want to finish reading that."

"Mrs. Farley won't let you check it out," Paula said. "And we're not going to sit here for an hour while Carl's team catches up with us."

Rick held out his hand. "Give it to me."

"What are you going to do?" Tracie asked.

"Sit on it," Rick said, leaning forward and sliding it under his rump.

"She'll see it," Tracie said. The paper stuck out the sides.

"She won't even look," Rick said. "People trust the handicapped. I bet a paraplegic could walk in and steal the 'Mona Lisa' from the Louvre and not a soul would notice."

"That would be something to see," Tracie said, getting the pun.

Rick smuggled the nineteenth-century newspaper outside without difficulty. But then Paula snatched it from under his bum and threw it in the Camaro's trunk, out of reach. She wanted him concentrating on getting them to Hawaii, she said. Making them millionaires could wait. Rick pouted all the way to the video store.

Movie Marvels was a brand-new store, and it was neat. Besides the finest selection of videos in town, it had tons of records, cassettes, and CDs. Of course, very few people in Express could afford a CD player, so they wouldn't be selling too many of those. They had wonderful posters; the walls were covered with them. Paula was a particular fan of dead rock stars and had their faces and bodies plastered all over her bedroom. Tracie's favorites were the guitar legends like Hendrix, Clapton, Page, and Van Halen. She was a fair guitarist herself. Yet, since no one in Express was able to afford musical instruments, either, she had never been in a band. It was probably just as well; the autobiographical footnote wouldn't have looked good on her application to medical school. Naturally, because he was dead, Paula had long ago stolen her poster of Jimi Hendrix.

It was as cold inside the video store as it had been inside the library. The store manager waved to them as if he were expecting them, but he was with a customer and didn't speak to them. They hurried over to the videos and almost screamed when they found a plastic Baggie taped to the shelf behind *The Empire Strikes Back*. Inside were a dozen thin gold chains, and a folded typed page listing the contents of the Baggie, and containing the clue: *"I could've been a contender."*

"Break out the suntan lotion," Paula cheered, placing the gold chain over her neck.

"Not so fast," Rick warned. "I don't know how this clue relates to 'At the best prices.'"

"Give yourself a minute, for godsakes," Paula said, chuckling.

"But all the others I got right away," Rick said, disturbed. "Does this line ring a bell with either of you?"

"No," Paula said. Tracie shook her head.

"It's been going too easily," Rick said, stretching his back and grimacing slightly.

"It'll come to you," Paula said.

"No, that's the thing," Rick said. "I also know I can't know it without knowing something else first."

"Look," Paula said. "Don't pressure yourself. I bet Tom hasn't even put on his sock yet. We have time."

A half hour later they had thirty minutes less time and Rick wasn't any closer to solving the riddle. It was then Carl and Tom strolled into the video store. They were alone, and Tracie was happy to see Carl even though it might mean she wouldn't be going to Hawaii. He smiled when he saw her, and he didn't often smile.

"We had a feeling we weren't in first place," Carl said.

"You're tied for first now," Tracie said. "Isn't this fun?"

"It's interesting," Carl said. He put a hand on Rick's shoulder. "How's my man?"

Rick looked embarrassed. "To tell you the truth, I'm stuck. Have a look at this." He led Carl and Tom to the *Star Wars* video. Tom took a chain out of the Baggie and put it over his head. He had yet to put the single white sock on. Carl studied the clue. "I don't want you to tell me what it means," Rick said. "Just tell me if you get it."

"I don't get it," Carl said.

"Where're Cessy and Davey?" Paula asked Tom.

"Cessy wanted ice cream," Tom said. "They're across the street."

"I love ice cream," Paula said to Tom. "Would you buy me a chewy chocolate cone?"

Tom lowered his eyes. "I don't have any money."

"Are you serious?" she asked in a slightly annoyed tone.

"Hey, old buddy," Carl said. "You need to borrow a few dollars?"

"I don't know," Tom mumbled.

"I wouldn't mind a strawberry shake," Rick remarked.

Tracie ended up going for ice cream for everybody. She wasn't sure how that happened. Carl and Rick wanted to discuss how they had cracked the previous riddles. They also seemed hesitant to leave the latest clue in case another team arrived; they wanted to know who their competition was. And Paula and Tom—Tracie didn't know why Paula stayed to talk to him when all she was doing was making snide personal remarks that he didn't understand. Some flirting.

But before Tracie could reach the ice-cream parlor, she saw something that made her sick to her stomach.

Cessy and Davey. They were sitting across the street in the front seat of Carl's truck. Cessy had two ice-cream cones in her hands. Davey didn't appear to have any. His mouth was nevertheless fully occupied.

He was kissing Cessy. On the lips. She was kissing him back. Sort of. In between kisses, she would hungrily lick both her cones.

CHAPTER
V

CARL WAS ABOUT TO GO LOOKING FOR TRACIE. SHE HAD been gone half an hour and he was worried about her. Neither Cessy nor Davey had seen her at the ice-cream parlor. But just as he was reaching for the video store door, he saw her through the glass crossing the road with ice cream. He stood by the door and waited.

"Where did you get to?" he asked, opening the door for her a moment later.

She smiled quickly. It was her trademark. She was such a pleasant girl. In all the years he had known her, he had not once seen her anything but friendly. But this smile—it was a trifle too quick. Something was bothering her.

"There was a line," she said.

He could see the inside of the ice-cream parlor from where he stood. There wasn't a customer in it. He let the door close and the cool air surrounded them. Tracie looked a tad pale and her hands trembled as she gave him the bag.

"What's wrong?" he asked.

"Nothing."

"You look upset."

"I'm fine. I got you a chocolate shake. They were out of vanilla. Is that all right?"

He glanced in the bag and frowned. "It looks like you got four chocolate shakes."

"Doesn't Tom like chocolate? Rick and Paula do. They'll eat anything. But I can take them back if you guys don't like them?"

"No," Carl said. "It's just that I thought Rick wanted . . . Never mind. As long as you're all right. I was worried about you."

"You were? I'm worried about you. I mean, thanks. Yeah, thanks, everything is all right. Where are Cessy and Davey?"

He gestured to the back of the store. "Over there. Where else would they be?"

"I was just wondering is all."

"Didn't you get yourself anything?"

"No." She looked past him. "My stomach's bothering me."

Carl handed out the ice creams. Cessy took Tom's shake. She said she was starving. Tom didn't seem to mind. Carl tried to pay Tracie for the ice cream, but she wouldn't hear of it.

Carl felt like Rick—stuck. No matter how many times he racked his brain, he couldn't relate the two clues. Surprisingly, Davey didn't appear to be straining over the matter, when it was Davey who had been largely responsible for cracking the previous clue about the hill on the cross-country course. He seemed content to tease Rick about his inability to solve the riddle.

"If you don't win this thing," Davey said to Rick,

"your reputation will be ruined. They probably won't even let you speak at graduation."

"If you win this thing," Rick said, "everybody will know you cheated, and your reputation will be secure. They'll probably flunk you and let you serve another term as senior class president."

"Touché," Davey said, laughing. He slapped Rick hard on the back, almost knocking him from his chair. "You kill me."

"I'm glad," Rick muttered, straightening himself. "I went looking for that article you told me about. I couldn't find it."

"Keep looking," Davey said.

"What paper was it in again?"

"I told you—last Sunday's *Times*. I think that was it."

"It wasn't."

Davey stared at him. "Did you find anything on Valta?"

Rick stared back at him. "No."

Davey smiled. "Keep looking," he repeated.

The big breakthrough didn't come for another thirty minutes. Even at that late an hour—it was getting close to one o'clock—no other team had put in an appearance. Carl was frankly amazed that nobody else in the school had solved the first three riddles. For all he knew, the others could be stuck on clue number one.

Rick probably should have been given sole credit for solving the blasted thing, although Tracie was the one who pinpointed the specific answer. They were all standing around squeezing their brain synapses— except for Cessy, who had gone for another shake—

when suddenly Rick asked his sister to open the video store front door so he could get a breath of fresh air. It was his inability to hide his excitement—and the fact that Express had no fresh air outside of an air-conditioned building—that let the cat out of the bag. When he came back in, he was grinning from ear to ear. Plus, he didn't ask Tracie and Paula to leave with him for another location. He just rolled over and started going through the records and the poster racks. It was then the truth dawned on Carl.

"The next location is in this store," he said.

"Really?" Rick asked, trying to sound casual, his face falling slightly.

"That's it," Carl insisted. "It has to be. The finest selection at the best prices. They go together."

Rick nodded, admitting defeat. "That is why I went outside. I wanted to check the big sign in the window. It says that. The connection between the lines was so obvious—I can't believe I didn't see it right away."

"You're too hard on yourself," Carl said. "This clue must be a line from another movie."

"That's likely. Unfortunately, it's not a movie I've seen."

"We could go through all the videos in the store," Carl said.

"I was going to do that as soon as you guys got bored and moved on," Rick said.

"Wait a second," Tracie said, showing the first signs of life since she had returned from the ice-cream parlor. "I know this movie. So do you, Carl. It played at the Silver Screen when we were freshmen."

"Shh," Paula said. "Don't tell him."

"He's going to know in a few minutes, anyway, if

they peek behind all the videos in the store," Tracie said. "Don't you remember, Carl? That's the night we bumped into each other."

Carl nodded. "It was a Sunday night. They used to play old classics then." He snapped his fingers. "Marlon Brando in *On the Waterfront.*" He put on the accent Brando used in the movie. " 'Remember that night in the garden? You came down to my dressing room and you said, "Kid, this ain't your night. We're going for the price on Wilson." You remember that? This ain't your night. My night—I could've taken Wilson apart. I could've had class. I could've been a contender . . .' "

Tracie laughed. "That was a great movie."

"Yeah," Carl said. "We had a lot of fun that night."

Tracie stopped and smiled. "Yeah."

Rick was displeased. "I think it's a disgrace Mr. Partridge chose a movie from another era."

"I agree," Davey said. "That old geezer."

They hurried to the appropriate video. Sure enough, there was a typed paper pinned to the shelf behind the store's single copy of the movie. Carl wondered what they would have done had someone checked out the movie earlier in the day.

The next item was another white sock. The socks weren't actually on the shelf; the paper directed them to a cardboard box hidden beneath the cassette racks. It was weird—these socks were all wet. Tom didn't seem to mind. He took one from the box, and the other one from his pocket that he had obtained earlier at the school stump, and put them both on. A fine sight he made without any shoes to go with them.

"Sexy legs," Paula said, mocking him.

"Thanks," Tom said.

The next clue was as strange as the wet socks. It read: *For terrible lizards.*

"A metal grave for terrible lizards," Paula said. "Sounds like a heavy metal album. Could this one be in the store, too?"

"I doubt Mr. Partridge would use the same trick twice," Rick said, yawning. Tracie put her hands on his shoulders and whispered something in his ear. He quickly shook his head. Carl assumed she had asked if he needed to rest. Carl hoped the hunt wasn't putting too much pressure on him. It was true what Davey had said—everyone expected Rick to solve the riddles first.

They bid the video store goodbye and went outside. Davey walked across the street to get Cessy. Carl had never seen a girl in his life who could eat so much and not get fat. He had been enjoying her company. She was like a kid in many ways. She had incredible energy. The most trivial things seemed to give her tremendous pleasure. For example, she'd been so taken with the artificial swans at the park that they'd had to restrain her from wading into the lake to have a closer look.

Tom went and sat in the back of Carl's truck. He didn't seem to mind the sun beating down on him, or the sting of the hot metal beneath his bare legs. Paula helped Rick into Tracie's Camaro, stowing his wheelchair in the trunk. Carl had heard Tracie's car sputtering around the parking lot at school. He had been meaning to tell her to bring it by his shop. It sounded in dire need of a ring job. Of course, she had offered to stop by and he told her not to bother.

He supposed he didn't want her meeting the jerks he worked with. Those guys would have tried to paw her. A few had been in the shop twenty years and had brake fluid between their ears. God help him if he followed in their footsteps.

"It's been an exciting day," Tracie said as he walked her to her car.

"And we're only half done," Carl said.

"Say goodbye to Tom for me," Paula called from the back seat of the Camaro. "Tell him he should drink hard liquor. It would give him an excuse."

"Don't mind her," Tracie said.

"See you, Carl," Rick said.

"Any ideas about the lizards?" Carl asked him.

"A few," Rick said. "I'll write you about them from Honolulu."

Tracie opened her door. "I guess this is goodbye."

"For the time being," Carl said. "Who knows? Maybe our paths will cross again before the day is over."

She smiled. "In a place without a beginning, without an end, where the waters flow hidden beneath an empty sky?"

For no reason, the line sent a cold chill through his body. Or maybe it was just the chocolate shake he'd drunk. He glanced across the street. Davey had hold of Cessy and was dragging her out of the ice-cream parlor.

"It's possible," he replied, thinking how some said anything was possible. He didn't believe those people. Too many times, the past sabotaged the future before it could be. It had a momentum all it's own. Either that or he had too long a memory.

"Carl," Tracie said suddenly. "Are you having fun?"

Cessy had asked the same question. "Yes. Are you?"

She smiled and brushed a strand of red hair off her cheek. She had shiny hair. It was nothing to get lost in like Cessy's, but it looked as if it would be soft to touch. He had almost brushed the hair away for her. She probably wouldn't have minded. Her hug caught him off guard.

"Take care of yourself," she whispered in his ear as her arms went around him. But she didn't give him a chance to hug her back. She held him for only an instant before scooting behind the wheel of the Camaro. She would hardly look at him then. She seemed to be having trouble getting the key in the ignition. He didn't know what to do or say, so he did nothing. Then the Camaro started and Rick waved goodbye and Carl waved back. They left in a hurry, and Carl was sorry to see them go. Yet he was also relieved they were gone, and that, too, he did not understand. He wasn't in competition with them. He would've loved to see Rick and Tracie get a chance to visit Hawaii. He simply felt that they would be better off not hanging around him for the rest of the day.

CHAPTER
VI

CARL AND HIS PARTY SOLVED THE NEXT RIDDLE BY DRIVing around town and throwing out whatever came to mind, regardless of how ridiculous it was. They went through every lizard connection they could think of, and if the truth be known, they didn't come up with many. Carl got fixated early on the idea of lizard shoes and dragged them to several shoe stores before giving into the general consensus that Express didn't carry such exotic footwear.

Eventually, though, they hit upon the idea of the most terrible of all lizards—the dinosaurs. Davey brought them up. After that, they were cooking.

"Dinosaurs," Carl mused, pulling his truck to the side of the road beneath a shady tree, wishing for the hundredth time he had air conditioning. The back of his shirt would have been soaked with sweat, had it not been as dry as it was hot. The perspiration literally evaporated the instant his pores exposed it to the air. He didn't know how Cessy—who was sitting between him and Davey—managed to stay so cool. "That could be it," he said. "The only trouble is we don't have any dinosaur bones in this town."

"Who says we have to stay in this town?" Cessy asked.

"No one," Carl admitted. "But I don't even know if the museums in San Diego have dinosaur bones. Not to mention the fact that they don't ordinarily keep them in metal graves."

"Do they have to be in bone form?" Davey asked.

"I thought I saw some live dinosaurs strolling around town the other night," Cessy said in her most helpful manner.

"A guy with dinosaur leather shoes was probably walking them," Davey added.

"It was an honest mistake," Carl said. He tapped the half-open window at his back. "Are you following this, Tom?"

"Oil," Tom said.

"What?" Carl said.

"Oil," Tom repeated.

"Dinosaur bones are a source of oil!" Davey exclaimed. "Way to go, Tom!"

"But that's not literally correct," Carl said, nevertheless impressed with the concept. "Most natural oil comes from the decomposition of microscopic plant and animal life. I read that in a book."

"Then it must be true," Davey said. "But what are the chances Mr. Partridge or his club members read the same book?"

Carl nodded. "All right. But where do we find oil in a—" He stopped. "An oil tank. That must be it. It's made of metal. What do you think, Tom?"

Tom nodded.

"Let's go there!" Cessy said, excited.

"Where?" Davey asked impatiently.

"I don't care where," Cessy said. "As long as they have food."

"There're several oil tanks in town I can think of," Carl said. "There's a couple outside of town. Where should we begin?"

"Let's go to the closest one and work our way out," Davey said.

It seemed a reasonable suggestion. Unfortunately, they probably should have done the reverse. They spent a full two hours searching the oil tanks in town and came up empty-handed. The heat made the wasted effort particularly grueling. It didn't matter how much Carl drank—he was always thirsty. He couldn't remember a hotter day. If Cessy hadn't been along for the ride, it would have been like being in hell.

When they had exhausted Express, they got on Highway 22, taking the two-lane road four miles out of town to a small deserted oil refinery. The place hadn't been in operation since Carl could remember. Dust, rust, and tumbleweed had taken over. Parking beside the sagging front gate and climbing out of his truck, Carl wondered if Mr. Partridge honestly expected anyone to win the scavenger hunt. The area was dead silent; not even a bird or insect could be heard.

"I bet this is the place," Davey said confidently, stepping toward the lock on the gate. "It reminds me of Mr. Partridge."

"Why do you say that?" Carl asked.

Davey tugged on the chain. "Why do you ask?"

"No particular reason," Carl said. "I was just thinking how little we know about the guy to waste the whole day trying to solve his puzzle."

Davey let go of the chain. "That's an interesting suggestion."

Carl didn't know he had suggested anything. "What?"

"That this might all be an elaborate hoax," Davey said.

Carl looked at him closely. "You think that's possible?"

Davey smiled. "It wouldn't bother me one bit if it was true."

"My brother loves a good joke," Cessy said.

"Are we going to go inside or what?" Tom asked.

"The faculty wouldn't let him get away with it," Carl said.

"He's such a character," Davey said. "He came out of nowhere. He'll probably go back there. Would he care what they say?"

"I think we should go inside," Cessy said. "It looks like a fun place."

Davey glanced at the rusty lock and chain. "Let's circle around."

They didn't have to go far to find a place where they could slip beneath the fence. Cessy didn't hesitate to get down in the dust and the dirt. Carl went before her and saw a lot of her brown legs as he helped her up on the other side. He still wasn't sure if she had on any underwear. She asked his help in brushing off. That was fun. Carl was pretty sure she didn't have any on.

There were four oil tanks at the rear of the refinery.

Carl felt a certain uselessness as they skirted the refinery's web of pipes toward them. These tanks were ancient; they had long ago lost their paint. He couldn't imagine they were anything but dry hollow husks.

He turned out to be correct. It made no difference. There was a cardboard box on top on the first tank they climbed. It was filled with twelve jungle green camping hats. The whole dozen made Carl figure they had got there before Rick. Tom grabbed a hat and put it on. He was still walking around in his socks. They were both filthy. The clue on the side of the box read: *The Peaks.*

"Two of a kind," Cessy added, reading from the list. "Where are there two peaks around here?"

It was too easy to solve. Perhaps Mr. Partridge figured he would give them a break on that end of it, since it would require a Herculean effort to climb the peaks. From the top of the tank, they appeared to be within walking distance, two sharp, almost identical hills devoid of any trace of vegetation. But Carl knew from past experience how deceptive distance could be out here, especially when an object stood alone, as did these twin hills. They were at least another five miles into the desert.

The desert—they were there already and he hadn't noticed. There was nothing between them and the sharp barren hills except lizards and thorns. He had once tried climbing them in seventh grade with Joe. They hadn't been able to reach the top.

"They're right there," Carl said, pointing, the heat rising off the ground in shimmering waves before his outstretched arm. It would be a chore to maneuver his truck to the base of the peaks. He almost felt like saying the hell with it right then and there. Of course, he was fooling himself. There wasn't a chance he would quit in front of Cessy.

"Neat," she said. "We get to go hiking."

He managed to bring his truck within a quarter-mile of the hills. He guaranteed himself new shocks in the process. The ground was rocky; he shot his old ones. The bumping up and down gave him a slight headache. He had to worry about Tom in the back with no cushion beneath his rump. But Tom just nodded his stoic head whenever Carl asked how he was doing.

When they climbed out of the truck, Davey brought up the idea that there was no reason why all four of them should hike to the top. In fact, Davey said only Carl and Cessy should go.

"Why us two?" Carl asked.

"It'll give you two a chance to talk," Davey said, plopping down on the ground in the truck's shadow, resting his back against a tire.

"And give you a chance to recuperate," Carl said. It was funny how he had never asked himself how he felt about Davey. He probably subconsciously recognized the fact he had to stay on his good side if he was to get anywhere with Cessy. But now that he thought about it, he didn't much care for the guy.

"Tom can't climb the hill without shoes," Davey said, closing his eyes. "Someone's got to stay and keep him company. Go ahead—take the water bottle. Cessy will keep your energy up."

"All right," Carl said, not feeling in the mood to argue. He seldom argued with anybody. That was one of his problems. Shielding his eyes from the sun, he looked up toward the top of the peaks, a steep fifteen hundred feet above his head, and prayed his legs didn't fall off. Cessy leaned over and whispered confidentially in his ear.

"I have a lot more energy than he does," she said.

The hike went well enough until they started up. Then it became murderous, and Carl was not out of shape. He had a clear-plastic gallon water bottle strung over his back, and with the sun beating down on it, they could have used its contents for making tea. There was no clear path up the hills, certainly nothing that gradually wound to the top. Not that it mattered. Cessy wouldn't have followed it. She was in a hurry to reach the summit. She believed in the straight and the true. She bounded forward in front of him, and his male ego demanded he not ask to take a break.

"What if it's the other peak?" she called over her shoulder.

"Let's not think about it," he said, panting. They had chosen the closer one because it was closer.

She glanced back at him and smiled. "Tired?"

"No."

"Having fun?"

"Yes."

"Wish you were back in my swimming pool?"

"Yes. Maybe when this is all over we can go for a swim."

She paused, glancing down at the truck, which already looked remarkably tiny. Neither Davey nor Tom were visible. Carl wondered what Tom thought of Davey. It was funny he had never asked him before. Cessy lost her smile. "We'll see," she said.

They had chosen correctly. There was a cardboard box at the top. It contained a pair of hiking boots. One pair. Cessy said they should take both of them. Carl plopped down on a nearby rock without even looking in the box, trying to catch his breath.

"Would that be fair to the others?" he asked.

"It says on the side 'a *pair* of hiking boots.' We have to take both. They might fit Tom." Cessy stepped to the edge of the peak and looked out, east, away from town. "He'll need something on his feet. I don't think we're going back to town."

"Why do you say that?"

"Because of the next clue. It says, 'Keep going.'"

"What did the clue on the list say?"

"All alone with nothing around." Cessy held out her arm. "Look, there's a small house out there all by itself. That's what it must be referring to."

Carl got to his feet with effort. He wondered if he could roll back down the hill. He could feel blisters forming on both his big toes. He stepped to Cessy's side.

It was an odd house. Besides being totally isolated, it was purple. Carl had never seen a purple house before. He had never heard of anyone living out there.

"I don't see a road leading to it," Carl said.

"I do," Cessy said. "It's a dirt road. It comes in from the back."

He squinted. "Your eyes must be sharper than mine."

"They are." She looked at him with her big dark-blue eyes. They were always dancing, always looking for fun—he hadn't noticed the intelligence behind them before. "I see a lot of things you don't."

He blushed beneath his sunburn. "What do you see?"

"That you're tired." She took his arm. "Come, let's sit. Let's talk."

She led him to the boulder he had plopped down on a moment ago and sat beside him, picking up the jug. "Thirsty?" she asked.

"Not for boiling hot water."

She pulled off the cap, inverting the bottle about a foot above her wide mouth and tilting her head back. She let it all pour out, swallowing at most a couple of ounces, allowing the rest to splash over the front of her dress, in her hair. She was not wearing a bra, and the drenching reminded him again how full her breasts were, how smooth ran the curve of her hips. As if he needed reminding.

"What are you thinking?" she asked as she set aside the bottle.

"Nothing."

"No. Your mind is never empty. Tell me."

"You mean you can't read my mind?"

She smiled, drops from the bottle still clinging to her cheeks. "I don't know you that well," she said. "Tom has only told me a few things about you. And I do not trust everything he says."

"What did he say?"

"That you were old friends."

"We are. We go way back. Did he say anything else?"

"A few things," Cessy said.

"How is it you and Tom became friends? You seem so different."

"We have things in common. It would surprise you."

"How did you meet him?"

"Through Davey. Davey likes Tom. He says he does."

Carl chuckled, remembering her remark at breakfast. "But you don't believe him?"

Cessy smiled again. "He's a liar. I should tell you that about him. But then, it runs in the family." She shifted her position on the rock so that the side of her leg touched his. He found the steadiness of her gaze intimidating. "Did you want to ask something else, Carl?"

"No."

"It's OK. Don't be embarrassed. I'm not shy."

He shrugged. "I was just wondering why you suddenly called this morning to invite me to be on your team?"

"Tom told me to."

"Oh."

"Davey also wanted me to call you," she said.

He chuckled again to hide his disappointment. "I'm glad somebody likes me."

She touched his arm. Her hand felt remarkably cool. "Somebody does like you. Do you know who?"

"Who?"

"Tracie."

"Huh? Oh, Tracie, yeah. We're old friends."

Cessy let go of his arm and looked away, frowning.

He had never seen her serious before. "No, it is something else. She doesn't like to see you. It causes her pain. But she *needs* to see you. That is what I see."

"I don't understand what you're saying."

She closed her eyes and put a hand to her head as if she might be the one in pain. "Yes," she said softly. "It's hard to understand."

"What is?"

"How she feels."

"You're imagining things if you think Tracie loves me."

Cessy suddenly opened her eyes and looked up. "I was going to use that word. Have you ever been in love?"

"Have you?"

"No. Is it fun?"

Carl laughed uneasily. "I've heard it can be very painful."

Cessy nodded faintly, watching him. "I believe you." She continued to stare at him. Then she casually stretched out a hand and touched the back of his neck, rubbing his tense muscles there, tugging lightly on his hair. She did it so suddenly, and yet so deceptively slowly, the action had him almost hypnotized. Then she moved close enough to where he could feel the clean coolness of her breath on the side of his face. She had such big lips. He stopped breathing when she leaned over and kissed him with them.

"Do you want to go back?" she whispered as she pulled back a moment later, nuzzling her nose into the side of his cheek. He wasn't sure what she was asking, or if he had even kissed her in return. He took a deep breath and swallowed. He should have been excited, and he was. Only he felt oddly heavy, as if he were about to sink into the rock they sat upon. Both her dark-blue eyes were wide open, her long black lashes gently brushing his skin.

"I'd like to see where the hunt leads," he said.

"So does Davey. So does Tom."

"Don't you?" he asked.

She moved away. He imagined for a moment he heard a sigh escape her lips. Then she flashed her usual bewitching smile.

"It could be fun," she said.

Their team did not reach the house until six o'clock. He and Cessy took their time going back down the hill. She was no longer in a hurry. She was showing no signs of fatigue, however. He couldn't understand it. She had the endurance of an Olympic athlete and the personality of a woodland sprite. Nothing about her made any sense. He felt so confused—like someone who had gone alone to bed in one room, only to awaken beside a stranger in another. Indeed, his confusion had started the moment *she* had awakened him. It had been a weird day.

Her kiss—it had tasted sweet as magic. But like a trick performed by a professional magician, there had been something insubstantial about it.

Why did she bring up Tracie?

He doubted it had been out of jealousy.

The dirt road Cessy had spoken of did exist. To get to it from the base of the peaks, they had to cross a wasteland of prickly tumbleweed, chipped rocks, and parched shrubs. Now he needed a new paint job as well as new shocks.

They parked ten yards shy of the front door.

"Should we knock?" Carl asked.

"Honk," Davey said.

"That would be rude," Cessy said.

Davey reached over and pressed the horn twice. No one came to the front door. "No one's home," he told his sister. "We didn't offend anybody."

They got out of the truck. The sun would set inside an hour, but it was still burning up the sky. The ground also held the heat. Carl's blisters had finished forming long ago and popped.

Tom had on the boots from the top of the hill. Now all he needed was a pair of pants to be fully dressed.

They found a pair of jeans in a cardboard box on the front porch.

Tom put them on. They fit nicely.

The clue said: *Keep going.*

"To where?" Carl asked, standing on the rickety front porch with the others. Someone had ripped several boards off the floor and nailed them over the front door and across the windows. That someone had been in a hurry. They probably could have broken into the joint without much effort, had they wanted.

But Carl did not want to. He did not like the feel of the place. It may have been the faint smell in the air. The surroundings were as dry as Sahara sand, yet he was reminded of a swamp, of putrid water and decaying fish. Where was the odor coming from? Whose house was this? Cessy sat on the porch railing, swinging her long brown legs in the warm pink light.

"To know where we should go," she said in jest, "we should first ask ourselves where we are."

Davey shook his head, pacing the porch, excited. "It

94

doesn't matter. We're closing in on our goal. Tom, don't you think 'Keep going' means we should continue along this dirt road?"

"Definitely," Tom said.

"How can you say definitely?" Carl asked.

"I just said it," Tom said.

Carl shifted uneasily. "If we stay on this road, we'll go deep into the desert. God only knows where it leads."

Tom looked at him. "You know."

"Not really," Carl said.

"Sure you do," Davey said. "You grew up around here. We have to go on. We have to go now. The others will catch us if we don't."

"I doubt that," Carl said.

"I wouldn't underestimate Rick or Tracie," Davey said seriously, stopping in front of Carl. He had the same eyes as Cessy. They were identical. They had the same hair. She said they were both liars.

"I don't know if I want to take my truck out there," Carl said.

Davey smiled, and *that* was different from Cessy. Her smile was rich with fun and laughter. There wasn't a trace of warmth in Davey's.

"Think of the grand prize," Davey said. "The Hawaiian islands. Floating in that warm blue water."

"I don't know," Carl said.

"We don't have any choice," Davey said.

He did say *we*. Carl heard him. Yet his mind understood it differently.

You don't have any choice.

Carl might have argued with Davey further if it hadn't been for the lizard. He didn't know where it came from, and when he first saw it, he had trouble believing his own eyes. It was the biggest lizard he had ever seen, two feet from head to hind leg, with a scaly tail that could have been skinned and stretched into a belt for a whole heavy metal band of Satan worshippers. He didn't recognize the species. It was the same color as the house. A purple lizard.

It had two claws on Cessy's right foot. It was ready to crawl up her leg. Cessy looked down at it and smiled.

"Hello," she said.

Carl reacted instinctively, jumping forward and lashing out with his right foot. The tip of his shoe caught the lizard on its jaw, barely grazing Cessy's skin. Unfortunately, the kick threw him off balance. He went flying along with the lizard. It hit the house wall to the right side of the door. He hit the wooden floor with his head. A sharp pain stabbed across both his temples. Rolling onto his side, he was presented with a mouse-eyed view of the lizard as it picked itself up and scampered toward his unprotected face, its dark purple tongue flashing.

"Tom!" he cried.

Davey stepped on it. On its head. He had on high black leather boots, and incredible reflexes and power in his legs. His sharp heel ground the lizard's skull flat into the floor with sickening finality. Black blood spurted over the splintered boards. The lizard's tail flopped twice and then lay still. Davey slowly raised his boot, revealing a pulpy mess. Carl closed his eyes, feeling sick to his stomach. He wasn't sure who yanked him to his feet. It must have been Tom. When he reopened his eyes, Tom had a hand on his arm, his face as impassive and masklike as that morning when he hadn't even bothered to glance over at Cessy's naked body.

"It's time to go, old buddy," Tom said.

They climbed in the truck. Tom got behind the wheel. Carl sat in the back. Before they drove away, he removed his watch and tossed it in the sand by the front porch. Dread was growing dark and heavy in his heart. The watch was a message in a bottle—a selfish gesture. He almost hoped the others didn't come far enough to find it.

CHAPTER
VII

In the Church

THE PRIEST HAD LISTENED CLOSELY WHILE THE BOY NARrated the details of the scavenger hunt. He'd asked several clarifying questions, and had seemed genuinely interested in the structure of the puzzle. But as the boy began to ramble on about the many clues, items, and locations, without relating them to his fears or his supposed crime, the priest began to lose patience.

"But when did you kill this person you spoke of?" the priest asked.

"A long time ago," the boy said.

"Why are you only now coming to confession?"

"I'm not here because of that. Don't you understand what I'm telling you? They're evil. They've got to be stopped. You've got to help me, Father."

"I can't help you, until you tell me what you've done. If you have murdered someone, we must start there. This scavenger hunt you've spoken of—it seems to me of no importance."

"No. It's very important. It was all a lie."

"How so?"

"It was only there to lead me back to that place."

"Where?" the priest asked.

The boy glanced nervously about the confessional cubicle. He wasn't sure where he was now. How could he say where he had been? He didn't understand why they had to make these booths so dark. The devil was supposed to like the dark. He placed his open palm on the stone wall on his right. It was thick, strong. They wouldn't be coming through that wall. He prayed the candle he had lit to the Virgin Mary was still burning.

"Where there's no beginning," the boy answered softly. "No end. Where the waters flow hidden beneath an empty sky."

"That was a riddle from your scavenger hunt?"

"It wasn't my hunt. It was theirs. They've been hunting me!"

"Why?"

"They need me. They need another victim."

"Why did they choose you?"

"Because I murdered my friend."

The priest sighed, his outline shifting behind the dark screen that separated them. The boy heard a clink of glass and wondered if the man had a bottle with him. Yet the priest did not sound anything but sober.

"You keep coming back to this murder you committed," the priest said. "And then you tell me it's not important. I can't stay here all night with you. Tell me what is important and let's be done with it."

"I haven't finished explaining the scavenger hunt to you. I have to do that first. Please?"

The priest sat back behind the screen, the shadow of his head going out of focus. "Very well, finish. You left the house and drove into the desert. What happened next?"

"We drove forever. Then we took a wrong turn. That was a joke. They thought it was funny. We drove some more, off the road. We came to this ravine. The moon came out. I could see it. But then we went into this place."

"Yes?"

A hot steel band tightened around the boy's chest. He had to close his eyes and fight for breath at the horror of the memory. "This terrible place," he whispered.

"Where was it?" the priest asked.

"Underground. A mine. No, it was a tunnel. It was very old. I think it's always been there."

"What happened when you went in there?"

"A sacrifice."

"Someone died?" the priest asked.

"Yes. Someone. A good friend."

"Who killed this person?"

The boy slowly opened his eyes. "They did."

"The people with you?"

"Yes."

"Why?"

"Father?"

"Yes, son?"

"Do you really believe Jesus came back from the dead?"

"I do. It's the cornerstone of my faith."

"Do you believe anyone else has ever come back from the dead?"

"The Bible describes how the Lord raised Lazarus from the grave."

"I'm not talking about what the Lord's done. I'm talking about ordinary people coming back. Have you ever heard about that?"

"You mean, without God's grace?"

"Yes," the boy said.

"No. That wouldn't be possible. Only God can give life."

"What about the devil?"

"He has no such power."

"Father," the boy said, beginning to tremble again. "I've got bad news for you."

CHAPTER

VIII

TRACIE'S TEAM DID NOT REACH THE PURPLE HOUSE UNTIL close to sunset. They had been beset with delays, but not from an inability to decipher the clues. Rick had solved the riddle about "a metal grave for terrible lizards" ten minutes after leaving the video store. It was about then he began to throw up. Paula thought it must have been the strain of running around in the heat. Rick thought the milk in the shake must have been sour. Then Paula thought Cessy's lipstick must have poisoned Rick's straw. Cessy had taken a hearty drink of Rick's shake while they were hanging out in the video store waiting for inspiration. But Cessy had not been wearing lipstick, and besides, Tracie thought, Paula was anxious to blame Cessy for anything. Paula was showing definite signs of becoming jealous of Cessy and Tom's friendship.

Naturally, Tracie could have put Paula at ease by telling her about Cessy and Davey's incestuous relationship. She had kept her mouth shut. She still felt uncomfortable thinking about it, never mind talking about it. Besides, it was none of her business. Tracie disliked gossips.

Yet she had almost told Carl before they parted in the video store parking lot. And she might have, except it would have sounded as lame as what she really wanted to tell him.

"I love you."

Neither, she was sure, would've impressed him.

Rick was sick for almost an hour. Despite his pleas for them to check out all the oil tanks in town while he barfed out his guts in private, they stayed with him, resting at Tracie's empty house, until he was able to move outside a twenty-foot radius of a bathroom. Unfortunately, they then made the tactical mistake of assuming Mr. Partridge had placed his next surprise in the oil tank closest to school, when in fact he did the reverse. Tracie thought there was no way they were closing in on Hawaii when they parked beside the deserted oil refinery two miles outside the city. Driving there had seemed an act of desperation. But the day was full of surprises. Standing on top of the empty oil tank only a few minutes after arriving, Tracie decided there was no way they could climb the Peaks.

She had been right there. *They* didn't climb anything—*she* did. Paula used the excuse that Rick shouldn't be left alone at the car, when Tracie would have been more than happy to stay with him. The only thing that kept Tracie from collapsing on the steep slope was the two sets of footprints leading her straight to the top. One belonged to a guy, the other had to be a girl.

While standing all alone on the summit of the hill, she first began to suspect there might be something wrong with a scavenger hunt that led them to such a forsaken place. But the thought came out of nowhere and didn't linger.

Carl and his pals had stolen all the boots from the cardboard box at point number seven, but were gracious enough to leave the clue. Now Tracie and *her* pals had a purple house to examine. It waited for them at the end of a bumpy road. The rough terrain was destroying her car. Dust flew off her hood as she brought her Camaro to a sudden stop close to the porch. Judging from the numerous footprints in the dirt, they were still in second place, maybe third or fourth.

"Who the hell would want to live out here?" Paula asked.

They got out of the car. Another few minutes and the sun would fall behind the horizon. The temperature was dropping swiftly, but it had a long way to go before it would be comfortable. Tracie wrinkled her nose at the foul smell in the air, wondering about its source. She was the first one to see the watch lying in the sand.

"Oh, no," Tracie said, kneeling down and picking it up.

"What's wrong?" Paula asked.

"This belongs to Carl," she said.

"So?" Paula said. "You can give it back to him when you see him."

"But the band isn't broken," Tracie said.

"Let me see it," Rick said. Tracie gave it to him, and after a brief study he muttered, "I can't see him dropping it on purpose."

"Unless he wanted us to know he'd been here," Paula suggested.

"Unless he was in trouble," Tracie said.

"That's ridiculous," Paula said.

"He might have set it down and accidentally left it," Rick said.

"Right," Tracie said. "He set it down in the sand." She began to pace anxiously. "I knew it. I knew I should have warned him."

"Don't you think you're overreacting?" Paula asked.

"No."

Rick was watching her curiously. "What's the matter?"

Tracie stopped her pacing. "It's nothing."

"What did you mean you should have warned him?" Rick insisted.

"Paranoia," Paula muttered, shaking her head.

"No, there's something," Tracie said. "At the ice-cream parlor—I saw Cessy and Davey kissing."

Paula snorted. "You're crazy."

Tracie stared hard at her. "I'm not."

"So they're lovers, and not brother and sister," Paula said. "So what?"

"Paula," Rick said patiently, "you're ignoring certain hereditary traits."

"Huh?"

"They look alike," Tracie growled. A cold breath brushed her anxiety. "They look *exactly* alike."

"Not exactly," Rick said. "Cessy has far more dynamic mammary glands." He considered further. "But I could swear they were twins."

"Let's check this house out," Tracie said, slipping Carl's watch on her own wrist.

The cardboard box on the front porch was empty. The typed paper taped to the side read, A PAIR OF BLUE JEANS, followed by the clue: *Keep going.* There was something else—a dark slimy trail that started at the center of the porch and dead-ended at the wall of the house. There was no body. Just the trail of black. Flies buzzed about it. More flies lay lifeless beside it.

"Is that blood?" Paula asked, grossed out.

"It's the blackest blood I've ever seen," Rick said, frowning. "Notice the dead flies. You'd think the stuff is poisonous."

"But the trail just stops," Tracie said. "What could have left it?"

"We might search the area and find out," Rick said.

"Let's not," Paula said. They looked at her. "This isn't a creature hunt, guys. What does this clue mean?"

"Probably what it says," Rick said. "It wants us to 'eep following this road."

"To where?" Paula asked.

"I suppose farther into the desert," Rick said.

"You mean, we're just supposed to keep driving?" Paula asked. "Until we see what? It's going to be dark soon. We'll get lost." She reached for a cigarette, fumbling with her lighter. "What do you think, Tracie? Tracie? What are you staring at?"

"What's that around your neck?" Tracie asked.

"A gold chain," Paula said, touching it with her hand.

"No," Tracie said. "You have two chains on. Did you take two from the video store?"

"No. Joe gave me this other chain. You know that."

Tracie felt the life slowly drain from her body. The feeling came before the reason, and even when her conscious mind pinpointed what was bothering her in the immediate vicinity, her heart knew she had only grasped the top branch of a huge buried tree, with roots as deep as they were rotten.

"The chains are identical," Tracie said.

"So?" Paula asked. "They're both thin. They're both cheap."

Tracie's eyes fell back to the black blood. Two more flies had conked out since they'd been watching. "How was Mr. Partridge dressed this morning?" she asked.

"Weird," Rick said. "He had on hiking clothes. But they were all gray."

"What kind of clothes have we been finding all day?" Tracie asked.

"Hiking clothes," Rick said, thoughtful.

"Since when do hikers wear gold chains?" Paula asked.

Tracie sat on the porch railing, not far from where the black trail began. "What have we been doing all day?" she asked.

"Dressing Mr. Partridge?" Rick asked.

"Yes," Tracie said. "But not exactly."

"Did he have a gold chain on?" Paula asked.

"I don't know," Tracie said. "But Joe did."

A flash of anger crossed Paula's face. "When he died? No, he didn't. He gave me this chain the night before he went hiking with Carl. Anyway, what does Joe have to do with any of this?"

"I don't know," Tracie said.

Paula threw down the cigarette she had just lit. "Let's get out of here. I'm sick of this hunt. If we want to go to Hawaii, we can save up our money and go."

"Now what's wrong with you?" Rick asked, probably thinking the heat had finally gotten to the two of them.

"Nothing," Paula snapped.

"You look scared," Rick said.

"I'm not scared," Paula said.

"I am," Tracie said.

"Tracie," Rick said. "I might be able to help you with your problem if you'd tell me what your problem is. Are you suggesting the scavenger hunt is a farce?"

"In a way."

"Why?" Rick asked. "Just because the items we've been collecting bear a resemblance to the organizer's clothes?"

"There are other things that have been bothering me," Tracie said. "For example, we were stuck at the video store forever, but not a single other team caught up with us."

"They probably couldn't solve the earlier clues," Paula said. "They didn't have my brother."

"Yeah, and I'm so smart," Rick said, trying to make light of the compliment.

"You are smart," Tracie said. "But there's a lot of smart kids at school. Who gave us our list at the orientation meeting?"

"Davey," Rick said.

"Did he give us the same one he gave the others?" Tracie asked.

"I'm sure he did," Rick said.

"How can you be sure?" Tracie asked. "Maybe our list began like the others, and then changed."

"But Carl's team has the same list as us," Rick said. "I saw it."

Tracie nodded. "It was the same. And we know Carl was here."

"What are you suggesting?" Rick asked again.

"That we are being led," Tracie said.

"That's dumb," Paula said. "We don't even know where we're supposed to go next."

"Tracie," Rick said. "Finding Carl's watch seems to have set your head spinning. You like him, sure—I do, too. But I'm sure he's fine. Let's be logical. Davey isn't even a member of Mr. Partridge's club. How can you talk of a plot? There's no connection between the two."

"We can't be sure there isn't a connection," Tracie said. "They both arrived in Express at the beginning of the school year. They're both unusual people. Mr. Partridge wears sunglasses he never takes off. Davey kisses his sister."

"Are you also suspicious of Cessy?" Rick asked.

"Yes. She made Carl join their team."

"I doubt she had to twist his arm," Paula said.

"Tom got Carl to join their team," Rick said.

"Tom's another one who bugs me," Tracie said "When did he first show up?"

"I don't know," Paula said. "A long time ago. He's been here longer than Davey and Cessy and Mr Partridge."

"Are you sure?" Tracie said. "I'm not. In fact, I can't remember him at all from last year. I hardly remember seeing him at school this year."

"He was there," Rick said.

"He's just quiet," Paula said. "He's . . ."

"He's what?" Tracie asked when her friend didn't finish.

"Nothing."

"What?"

"Nothing." Paula strode to the edge of the porch and stared out across the desert, following the curve of the dirt road, the final orange rays of the setting sun slipping off her face. "Do you really think they're out there?"

"Yes," Tracie said. Rick was right—Paula was scared, much more than herself. But why? Tracie had to ask herself. Rick was right—the reasons she had given him were really no reasons at all. Kissing siblings, gray hiking clothes, lost watches, identical gold chains—it certainly didn't add up to the end of the world.

Tracie had a headache. She realized the bad smell was giving it to her. The odor appeared to be coming from inside the house.

"We'd never find them in that desert," Paula said. "They couldn't even find Joe."

"That's where he died, isn't it?" Tracie asked.

"Somewhere out there." Paula sighed. "Soon it'll be a year."

"I know," Tracie said. "It was last June that . . ." She paused. "When exactly will it be a year?"

Paula looked at her. "I can't remember."

"June fifth," Tracie said. "That's today's date, and it's a Friday." She closed her eyes, straining to go back. "Last year Joe and Carl went out on a Thursday. I remember. Joe was saying how he was going to miss some test, and that he didn't care." Tracie stopped and opened her eyes. "He died exactly a year ago today."

"What does Joe have to do with any of this?" Rick asked, exasperated. Tracie climbed off the porch railing.

"Rick," she said. "Whose house is this?"

"I have no idea. Probably no one's."

"I want a look inside before we leave," Tracie said. "I have a crowbar in my trunk—we can pull off these boards. But first let's go back to when we were walking from the track to the stump. Davey insisted we walk together. In fact, he flat out told us the next location so that we would have an excuse to go with him. Then he brought up that story about that gold mine. He directed it specifically at you, Rick."

"So? He thought I would find it interesting."

"Davey has hardly spoken to you the entire year," Tracie said. "And now he's suddenly interested in entertaining you. I find that suspicious. No, I think he was trying to tell you something."

"What?" Rick asked.

"I'm not sure. But he pointed you toward Mrs. Farley's records and you studied them for ten minutes and what did you find? An old newspaper with a story on Valta. Don't you think that's an amazing coincidence?"

Rick considered a moment. "I was surprised to find

something on the mine so quickly." He frowned. "That paper—it was right on top of the most obvious stack. Are you saying Davey planted it there?"

"Possibly," Tracie said. "Another thing. You couldn't find the article Davey was talking about. He was extremely vague about what paper it was in. I don't even think there was such an article."

"Why didn't you mention your suspicions before?" Rick asked.

"I didn't know he was kissing his sister then. And Carl hadn't left his watch behind for us to find yet."

"Why would Davey plant the paper?" Rick asked.

"Maybe to point you—or all three of us— somewhere else. Paula, you threw that paper in the trunk, right?"

"Yeah. I'm sure it's still there."

"Before we look at it," Rick said, "you might want to consider something else. Cessy didn't want Davey talking about the mine."

"How do you know?" Tracie asked.

"It was the look she had on her face," Rick said. "I was closer to her than you. Also, remember how she said she threw out his paper on purpose? She was mocking him, in a way. She wasn't acting like someone who was in on a secret plot."

"I'll keep that in mind," Tracie said, climbing off the porch, heading for the car. She had the paper in her hand a minute later. It was thin, a single yellowed page folded over—all text and no photographs. Yet it was remarkably well preserved.

It was dated June 5, 1862.

"That date is a hell of a coincidence," Rick had to admit when Tracie handed him the paper. With Tracie and Paula peering over his shoulder, the three of them read the article that started in the lower right-hand corner of the front page and continued onto the back.

FOOL'S GOLD
By Michael Hall

Gold fever struck Mark Sanders and James Westfall at an early age. They were only eighteen when they left a comfortable life in Chicago and headed west in search of their fortune. Lady Luck appeared to shine on the two best friends even before they reached California. In Denver they teamed up with a young couple carrying a map to a rich gold vein: Daniel and Claire Stevens. The Stevenses said they were looking for a couple of strong backs. The four entered into an agreement to split whatever they found equally. Sanders and Westfall figured they had nothing to lose. The Stevenses were covering all expenses.

The map led them to the deserts of Southern California. It gave precise directions. The group knew exactly where to dig. Within a week, they broke in upon an underground cave, a cave that led deep into the earth, to unimaginable riches. They found gold bars stacked everywhere. It didn't take them long to fill their leather sacks. Then, happy and excited, they headed north to San Francisco. They stayed in the finest hotels, dined at the best restaurants. They had their whole lives in front of them and money to do whatever they wished.

But they wanted more. Leaving their earnings safe in a bank vault, they returned to the cave. There they explored further into the earth. They were deep beneath the surface when they heard the deadly rumble of a cave-in at their backs.

They were trapped. They had no food, no water. Almost as bad, they had precious little oil for their lamps. Taking one of the lamps, the Stevenses left Sanders and Westfall to explore deeper for a way out. As the darkness began to close in upon the two young men, Mark Sanders managed to jot down a few last entries in his diary.

I don't know what day it is. I don't suppose it matters. It must be the third or the fourth. We have been in here forever. Claire and Dan have been gone a long time. Jim thinks they must have run out of oil and got lost in the dark. Here, near the entrance, the cave is straight and narrow, but deeper, it twists and turns in many directions. I pray I see them again before I die. I must see Claire once more. I feel I have to say goodbye, and tell her how sorry I am that it had to end this way.

Jim says we have to put out the light. We are both so tired. Could the air be going already? I have to sleep.

It is later. Jim is still resting, but I find it difficult to keep my eyes closed. I waste more of our oil. We are down to a single flask. I wish to God I had brought more.

I had a strange dream a little while ago. It was about Claire. She had returned with Dan to tell us of a way out that the two of them had found. They wanted Jim and me to go with them. But all they led us to was a narrow passageway that ended at a stone wall. In the dream, when Jim and I turned to ask Claire and Dan what they were doing, they told us to press against the wall, which we did. But our hands slipped into the rock and we couldn't get them out. I couldn't understand it. Our hands were frozen and it was terrible. Dan and Claire started laughing. Their laughter woke me up.

I don't know how late it is. I had another dream. I think it was a dream, but I also thought I was awake. I'm confused. It's very dark in here. It's getting colder. I have to stomp my feet on the ground to keep the life in them.

I saw Claire. She was returning from her exploration, without Dan. It had to be a dream. She had on a white dress, and I know she didn't bring a white dress with her. But she looked real. She told me it wouldn't be long now. When I asked her what she meant, she smiled and said I would be going swimming soon. Then she held out a cup of water for me to drink. I've been needing a drink for a while now. My throat is parched, and I've been coughing. I raised the cup to my lips. But it smelled odd, and when I dipped my hand in it to test it, my finger got burned. I don't know how this could be. Seeing that I wasn't going to drink it, she snatched it out of my hand and ran away. I would have followed her, but I couldn't get my legs to move. They were numb. Then I went to sleep, or maybe I just woke up. I don't know. All I know is the finger I dipped in the water in my dream is still hurting. It's all red.

Where is Claire? Who is she?

I think I've been sleeping again. A long time must have gone by. I feel much weaker. Jim spoke to me a few minutes ago, but now he has dozed off. I have no one to talk to. I feel so lonely.

What are Jim and I doing here? I know we are here to die, but how did this happen to us? I've been thinking a lot lately. I should have done so long ago. We were fools. We found the gold bricks and never stopped to ask who had made them, or how Claire and Dan knew where to find them. All Jim and I thought about was how wealthy we were.

This isn't a natural cave. It can't be. Most of it is walled in by stone and dirt, but there are portions as straight and smooth as a tunnel. This place must be old, older than the Indians. Maybe older than man. But someone constructed it. I remember a remark I made to Jim when we were prying the gold bricks from that cul-de-sac, how the place reminded me of an altar. Jim laughed at me, but our partners exchanged looks. They didn't think it was so funny.

They never told me why they called this place Valta.

I've had a change of heart. I don't want Dan and Claire to come back.

We should never have come to this place.

* * *

Jim is dead. It's horrible. I awoke not long ago and found him sitting up beside me. He had his hand on my shoulder. I called to him, but he didn't answer. Then I lit our lamp.

I feel I may be sick. His lips, his tongue—his whole mouth has been burned away. Half his face has melted over his shirt. It couldn't have happened long ago. The blood is still dripping out. His eyes are open. From the look in them, I think he was trying to scream when he died.

I know she did it to him. I know she offered him her poisonous drink. I should have told Jim about my nightmare. She must have come when the lamp was off. I remember how she and Dan always wanted us to carry the lamps. I don't believe they care much for fire.

I know they're alive, somewhere down there.

She was my friend. We worked together, we ate together. We even celebrated together. But I think she and her husband were celebrating something different from Jim and me. They gave us a day in the sun with all the money in the world and now they're killing us in this black hole.

Have I gone mad? I am confident that I have not. But if someday someone finds this diary, I'm afraid they will think so. That will probably be years from now. They will find our bare bones and say time has had its way with our remains. They will not see Jim's face as I see it now. They will not know that it did not take years for the flesh to fall from our bones, but minutes.

I pray I'm dead before Claire takes me swimming.

I have to stop now. The oil has run out. And I think I hear something. Oh, God, help me . . .

It's footsteps.

They're coming for me.

That was Mark Sanders's last entry. His diary was found on him approximately a year later. Even though he had been buried under ground the whole time, away from rodents and wild animals, there wasn't a speck of flesh left on his bones, nor were his clothes anywhere to be found. He was discovered propped up against a wall, beside a second skeleton. Both of them had their hands and arms arranged in a cruel gesture of welcome.

If time and circumstance permit, a second article on Claire and Daniel Stevens's gold mine will appear in this paper. The matter is still being researched.

"Well?" Tracie said when they were done reading.

"It's interesting," Rick said. "I had only begun the diary when I was interrupted at the library."

"Interesting?" Paula asked. "You're sick. It's horrible."

"My physical disability may be affecting my mind," Rick agreed.

"I want to know," Tracie said impatiently, taking the paper back from Rick, "how this article can be related to our present situation?"

"I would say there is no relationship," Rick said.

"Then why did Davey want you to read it?" Tracie demanded.

"I'm not fully convinced he did," Rick said. He raised his hand when she began to protest. "But I do agree with you that this isn't your normal haunted gold mine."

"Go on," Tracie said.

"This should have occurred to me at the beginning. You don't find gold mines this far south. Prospecting back then was usually done in the Sierras, north of Yosemite. Then, if we take as fact what the reporter has written, we run into all kinds of unexplainable phenomena. The gold taken from this mine obviously wasn't something they dug out of the ground. It was in neat bricks, Sanders said. Also, Claire and Daniel Stevens appear to have been carrying sulfuric acid in their canteens. They were not your typical prospectors."

"I received the impression the acid was from the mine itself," Tracie said. "Anyway, what else struck you as odd?"

Rick shrugged. "The entire article is odd. The person who wrote it doesn't say if he has been to the mine or not, or how he got hold of the diary. He ends the article awfully abruptly."

"As if he were in a hurry to send it off before he went back there," Tracie said thoughtfully. "Who is this Michael Hall? Could he be the president of the bank Davey referred to?"

"It's possible," Rick said. "The article didn't have to be written by a staff reporter." He stopped and stretched his back. "But what are we talking about here? Ghosts? How can we take any of it seriously?"

"Claire and Daniel Stevens," Tracie whispered, studying the paper, feeling dread settling over her again. "Cecilia and David Stepford."

"What was that?" Paula asked, still tense.

"Tracie," Rick said, smiling.

"How do you explain that the date on the paper matches today's date?" Tracie snapped.

"By agreeing with you," Rick said. "Say Davey not only planted the paper, but wrote it as well."

"What for?" Tracie asked.

"As a practical joke," Rick said. "To spook you and Paula. You could get something like this printed up anywhere. It wouldn't take an expert to make it look a hundred years old."

"Why would he tie his joke to the date Joe died?" Tracie asked. "He didn't even know Joe."

"That bastard," Paula said.

Rick was studying her. "Before the coincidence of the dates was even brought up, Tracie, you were talking about Joe. You never told me why."

Tracie stared at the trail of black blood and the dead flies. That gook smelled as if it had sulfuric acid in it. Her headache was getting worse.

"I don't know why," she said. "But there were four of them back then. Three guys, and one girl. A couple, and two friends. Like Carl's team today." She shook herself, glanced at the house. "We're breaking into this place."

"That could be against the law," Paula said.

"Since when do you care about the law?" Rick asked.

Paula came and stood beside her. "Tracie, let's just get out of here. It'll be dark soon. I'm not feeling well. I'm sure Rick's right—Carl will be OK. Come on, let's split. I don't want to go in there."

Paula was practically begging her, and Paula could ride on the back of a motorbike at a hundred miles an hour through every red light in town and not bat an eye. Tracie reached out and touched the two gold necklaces Paula wore. They were so thin—it would have been easy to wind them together and pretend they were one.

Paula was right—it would be getting dark soon. A black cloud could have drifted over their heads in the few minutes since the sun had gone down.

"We can't go," Tracie told Paula, taking back her hand.

"Why not?"

"Because even when I rack my brain, I can't think of a single instance when Tom was there last year," Tracie said.

"He's a nice guy." Paula's lip quivered. "I feel like I know him."

Tracie nodded. "So do I."

Rick didn't say anything. Tracie gave him back Michael Hall's article. She fetched the crowbar from her trunk when she had picked up the paper. Looking closer at the house, it seemed the paint had been thrown on the rough boards. The purple did not hide the age of the wood. It looked like a house from a ghost town that could have scared away all the ghosts.

Both the front door and the windows were boarded up, but the latter had been done far more carelessly. Tracie approached the window at the left of the door and slipped the crowbar under the top board. It was relatively new, unpainted and pierced with fresh nails. The plate glass beneath it was covered with enough dirt to pass for earth. With the others watching silently at her back, Tracie yanked upward. The screech of the nails made her jump. She hadn't realized how tense she was.

There were three boards. She dealt with each quickly and efficiently. Once the window was exposed, however, she couldn't see a way to open it from the outside. She hesitated only a moment before putting the crowbar through the glass. Even Rick jumped this time, and Paula ran to wait by the car. She should have known she would be going in alone, Tracie thought. Reaching past the jagged glass, she managed to undo a metal latch and pull the window up.

The front of the house faced dead south; the light in the west was almost useless. It was dark inside. Tracie called to Paula to bring her the flashlight from the glove compartment. As she raised her leg inside the window, the light tucked in her belt, Rick told her to shoot first and ask questions later. He was joking. She smiled and told him not to leave without her. Her heart refused to stop pounding.

The place stank. She could not specifically relate the smell to any she had encountered before, but it had a definite acidic edge. Straightening up, she stood perfectly still while her eyes adjusted to the gloom. She told herself she was afraid to cut herself on the glass, but she was just *afraid*. She had forgotten she had a flashlight. Pulling it out of her belt, she almost dropped it.

Naturally, the blasted thing needed new batteries. The beam came out weak and yellow. She played it over the room, the age of the interior reflecting the same deterioration as the outside. The ceiling was open to the beams, a mess of splinters, and the loosely fitted floor was waiting to trip her. There were no electrical sockets, no light switches. A square wooden table stood in the center of the room beside a frail chair that couldn't have supported a fat cat. Stepping toward it, the soles of her shoes left footprints in a grainy layer of dust.

A collection of newspaper articles lay neatly arranged atop the table. Someone could have been preparing to paste them in a scrapbook. The papers did not appear old. Tracie pressed the flashlight close to the article captions, sucking in a tight breath as she realized their subject matter.

THIRTEEN-YEAR-OLD CINDY POLLSTER
FOUND GARROTED

POLICE SUSPECT KIDNAPPING
IN TERRANCE CASE

COUPLE FIRST TIED TO BED
AND THEN STABBED TO DEATH

YOUNG NEWLYWED WAS SKINNED ALIVE

The papers did not appear old because they weren't. All the crimes had occurred in the last year in a circular pattern that had Express for a center. Tracie only had to read a few lines of each crime article to see that each involved horrible torture.

Who would collect such clippings?

The person who had done the torturing?

Get out of the house—now. Before it's too late.

But she couldn't leave, not with the others waiting outside for proof of something she couldn't even put into words. She glanced at the dial on Carl's watch. The hour and minute hands glowed in the dark. They said it was getting late. She collected the clippings and stuffed them in her pocket.

The wall before her, to the side of a black hallway, reminded her of the dirt-caked window she had shattered moments ago. Touching it, she realized why. It was glass, filthy glass, a mirror that ran from the floor to the ceiling.

Wiping away a circle of dirt, a face jumped out at her.

"Eeeh!" Tracie said, making a strangled sound.

She dropped the flashlight. It went off.

The face vanished.

Too late.

Her heart stopped pounding. It stopped beating—period—and the blood backed up inside her brain and her thoughts exploded in a million directions from an insane core. She would have dashed from the house if she'd had the wits. Pure terror consumed her.

For a moment. Then she understood. It was a mirror. She had shone her light directly into it. She had seen a reflection of something behind her. And it was a some*thing* and not a some*one* because the house was empty. She prayed it was empty as she bent, trembling, and collected her flashlight. It went back on and she mentally apologized for getting mad at it a moment ago because its batteries were weak. She shone the light away from the mirror.

Pinned in the center of the wall not far from where she had broken in was a life-size poster of Mr. Partridge. He had on his black sunglasses and was dressed in charcoal gray hiking clothes. He was smiling, which he seldom did in real life. She couldn't imagine what he was smiling about and didn't want to try. He looked sick as ever. She could see every bone in his pale face.

She realized this must be his house.

But that could not be possible. There was nothing but a table and chair. A glance toward what appeared to be the kitchen had already told her there wasn't even a stove, never mind food or water, the basics that normal people needed to live.

But did Mr. Partridge live on food?

A poster of the man smiling at himself in a filthy mirror.

Strange. Very strange.

It was then Tracie spotted the trail.

It seemed to be made up of the same black gook as outside. The trail started against the far wall of the kitchen and made a right turn into the living room before disappearing down the hall. Tracie stepped into the kitchen, passing through a cobweb, and shone the light on the floor.

The gook literally came out of the wall.

It came out of the wall exactly where the trail outside had disappeared into the wall.

Now for the bonus question. Am I going to follow it?

She was by no means isolated. Rick and Paula could not have been more than fifty feet away. Yet she felt totally alone. She could neither see nor hear her friends. And there was a quality about the interior of the house that cut it off from the outside. She had the impression that if she were to call out they would not hear her. They had not responded to her cry a moment ago. It was as if she stood in another time, another dimension.

In the end, she made no conscious decision. She simply started to follow the trail for a few feet, and then followed it a few more feet, and so on. In less than a minute she was heading down the hallway, the dark walls seemed to narrow with each step she took forward. The slimy gook got thicker, smoking faintly, and the pain in her head worsened, causing her vision to blur.

The trail led to the last door on the left. A single inch separated the bottom of the door from the floor.

That had presented no obstacle for the creature. It had simply kept going.

"This isn't a creature hunt, guys."

What was she following? And what could it possibly have to do with Davey and Cessy? She had been slow to ask herself those questions, and all of a sudden, she had to wonder if she honestly wanted to know. Strange company she could deal with. Creatures that bled something other than blood were different. The smell deepened her doubts. She had found its source. It was coming from the other side of the door.

From something inside the room.

She heard a scraping sound and pressed her head to the door.

Something still alive.

It sounded small and it sounded hurt. It could have had a tail. Besides scratching the floor, it was flopping all over the place. She listened closer.

Oh, God, help me. . . . They're coming for me.

Her light went out.

Blackness. Utter horror. Impossible to even scream.

The thing was dragging itself toward the door. She could smell it and it could smell her. It was probably hungry.

Why had her flashlight chosen that exact moment to fail? She had dropped it again. Falling to her knees, she desperately searched for it, a part of her brain shouting that she didn't need it to run back up the hall and jump out the window, a smaller, more persuasive portion of her mind whispering that a second bigger creature might have already blocked the way back to the window, and could be waiting behind her with open maw and razor-sharp teeth.

Her fingers banged the light. She flipped it on.

A fresh, thick glob of black blood oozed from beneath the door. Touching the tip of the flashlight, it instantly burned through the plastic and began to eat at the wood beneath. A loud bang hit the door, causing it to buckle.

The creature wasn't that small.

Tracie grabbed the flashlight and ran. Nothing ate her on the way out. She was fortunate she didn't cut open her head climbing out the window because she certainly wasn't watching for sharp glass. She was only watching her tail. Hopping onto the porch, the hot dry desert air hit her like a refreshing ocean breeze. She had not realized how suffocating the house had been. She bounded past Rick and stopped only when she reached the shrubs on the far side of her car. It was there she vomited.

"Are you all right?" Paula asked a minute later, standing beside her brother, the two of them worried.

No, I'm not so good. There's a monster in the house that collects Mr. Partridge posters and obscene articles. It almost slobbered on me. Don't go in there. The thing is from another planet, you've got to believe me.

"I'm fine," she whispered. If she told the truth, Rick would laugh at her. If they were lucky. He might want to go inside. She would have to tell him later, when they were far from this place.

"What happened?" Rick asked.

She straightened herself. "Nothing."

"What's in there?" Rick insisted.

"It's Mr. Partridge's house," she said.

"Are you sure?" Rick asked.

"I saw his picture on the wall."

"It must have been an awful picture," Paula said.

"You can't imagine," Tracie said, turning to follow the dirt road as it wound deep into the desert. Keep going, it said. Very well, they could play their game a while longer. Especially since it was the only game in town. She prayed to God Carl was all right.

"What are we going to do now?" Paula asked.

"We're going to follow this road," Tracie said.

"No," Paula said. "I can't."

"Yes," Tracie said firmly. "You must."

"How far?" Rick asked. "We won't find them."

"Till we reach the place where Joe died." Tracie stepped toward her car. "We'll find them. Davey must have planted that paper. He must want us to find him."

CHAPTER
IX

CARL HAD NEVER RIDDEN IN THE BACK OF HIS TRUCK before. It was far from comfortable. The bumps in the dirt road were doing a number on his spine, while the handkerchief he held to his mouth wasn't doing much to keep the dust out of his lungs. He wished Tom would slow down or, better yet, turn around and head back to Express. Twice Carl had banged on the window, only to be ignored. He probably would have been offended if he hadn't been so frightened.

"It's time to go, old buddy."

Tom had never spoken to him that way before. It hadn't even sounded like Tom. It had sounded like an order.

Then there was the purple lizard. Cessy had greeted it like an old friend. Davey had not been surprised to see it, either. But Carl had never seen a human being move as fast as Davey had when he had crushed the lizard's head beneath his boot. For an instant, Davey had appeared to be in two places at once.

Carl knocked on the window again. Cessy turned and waved to him. She turned away before he could speak. He glanced at the desert to either side of the road. Sand and weeds in a black land. Jumping wouldn't get him too far. He looked up at the stars—hard bright points in a moonless sky. At least the sky wasn't empty.

They would have to go through point nine to get to point ten.

He wasn't looking forward to going to Hawaii anymore.

They came to a halt an hour later. Carl didn't know where they were: California, Arizona, maybe Mexico. They had ridden at least sixty miles and hadn't passed a single car or dwelling—not easy to do anywhere in the U.S. Vague outlines of tired hills surrounded them on all sides; scattered Joshua trees stood like sentinels, their cactus arms frozen forever in uncomfortable upturned positions. Carl jumped down. His friends climbed out of the front. He could hardly see them.

"What are we doing out here?" he asked angrily.

"Having fun," Davey said. He flipped on the flashlight in his hand, shone it across the low wooden sign that stood to the front and left of the truck. Two words were scrawled on it in big red dripping letters:

WRONG TURN

A cardboard box sat under the sign. Davey gestured for Carl to check it out. Carl didn't want to. The three of them were waiting for him with expectant expressions; even Tom, who hadn't shown a flicker of interest in anything since he had gotten flattened in that football game. Or had the injury happened in a car accident? Suddenly Carl couldn't remember, and that troubled him as much as what he might find in the box. From where he stood, he could see the item was as dark as the letters on the sign.

"What is it?" he demanded.

"How should I know?" Davey asked.

"Cessy?" Carl asked.

She grinned but said nothing.

"Tom?" Carl asked, a faint note of pleading in his voice. Tom's next remark almost floored him.

"I never got hurt playing, Carl."

"What?"

"You just imagined it, Carl."

"B-but your head," Carl stuttered. "You hurt it. You haven't been the same since."

"He's the same," Davey said and chuckled. "Look in the box. We have to get down to business."

Carl looked. There was one shirt, a torn and weathered brown Pendleton caked with dried blood. His old friend came up at his side. Carl recoiled in horror when Tom reached down and picked it up and pulled it over his own head.

"Tom!" he cried.

"It fits him perfectly," Davey said, pleased. "What's the next clue? We've got to keep going if we want to win."

It was taped to the side of the box: *You should know by now.*

"What does it mean?" Carl asked, crouched on his knees beside the typed page. Cessy let out a hearty laugh.

"Oh, Carl," she said.

"It means my sister is driving," Davey said, turning

back to the truck, also laughing. He snapped off the flashlight. The full weight of the night returned.

"No," Carl said, straightening himself. "I want to go home."

An incredibly powerful hand grabbed the top of his arm. Carl could not believe it was his friend, until his friend spoke.

"No, Carl," Tom said.

Carl tried to shake loose. He could have been caught in the grip of a bear trap. Tom dragged him toward the truck and threw him in the back, climbing in beside him. Cessy turned the key and revved the engine. They jerked off the dirt road into the wasteland. Davey leaned his head out the window and howled at the sky. Cessy left the lights off and pressed the accelerator to the floor. Had Tom not been holding him flat against the truck bed, Carl would surely have bounced out the back.

They drove for about half an hour, long enough for Carl to realize that these people were no friends of his, and that they were probably going to kill him. The realization led to an equally disturbing insight—it was possible to wake up from a nightmare and have it continue into the day. He had only to glance at Tom's impassive expression to know this was true. In his dream of the dam and the flood, Carl had seen a similar expression on the face of the monster.

Similar. Yet not the same. Tom was not the monster that had swept toward him above the torrent. Or if he was, he continued to wear a mask. His best friend Tom. Why couldn't he remember the specific game when Tom got hurt? He couldn't have imagined the whole thing. They were talking about the structure of a life here. He and Tom had discussed the accident at length many times.

Of course, no one else had joined in their discussions. No one else ever talked to Tom—period. Except Cessy and Davey.

Carl decided they were all mad. Himself included.

But that didn't mean he was ready to die. Far from it. The thought of death terrified him. He had to escape. He had to think. What was he dealing with here? Were they even human? Each had displayed unusual abilities and characteristics. Cessy had eaten ten pounds of food since they had begun the scavenger hunt. Davey had blinding speed. And a stick of dynamite couldn't have burst the grip that Tom had on his wrists. What did that add up to? Vampires that were sick of blood? If she hadn't had her ice cream before they kissed, he decided, Cessy probably would have bitten his tongue off. Then again, she might have been trying to warn him on the hill.

"Do you want to go back?"

A simple "Get the hell out of here" would have been better.

"You people are weird," he told Tom.

Tom didn't respond, except to tighten his grip to the point where Carl felt real pain. Carl didn't complain, however. He didn't want to give the two up front anything else to laugh about.

When they finally did stop, Tom let him go. The blood poured back into Carl's hands and he sighed with relief. They'd gone farther up into the hills. The Joshuas were gone. A milky white light shone on the eastern horizon. The moon would be up soon. Climbing out of the truck, Carl was struck by how familiar the place looked. The savage landscape was primordial. A prehistoric beast could have raised its head over the ridge and Carl wouldn't have been surprised.

"Where are we?" he asked.

"Rust Valley," Davey said, walking slowly toward him with an object that looked amazingly like the rifle Carl stowed in the locked tool chest at the back of his truck for the rare occasion he went target shooting.

"But the individual who researched Valta put together enough facts to figure the mine must lie approximately fifty miles east of here, near Rust Valley."

"Are we going prospecting?" Carl asked, glancing at Cessy, who had her head turned in the direction of the moon, the faint light giving her ordinarily tan skin an otherworldly transparency.

"Not exactly," Davey said, coming closer. "We already know where the treasure is. We just want you to do a little digging for us."

"Sorry," Carl said. "I don't work for free."

Had Carl any doubts about Davey's inhuman reflexes, Davey answered them for him in a flash of movement that left Carl bent over on his knees on the ground and choking his guts out. Davey had reversed the rifle and rammed the butt end into Carl's diaphragm. Carl had never known such agony in his life. His heart and lungs felt as if they would burst. Davey lightly tapped the side of Carl's head with the barrel.

"Don't worry," Davey said. "We'll give you something for your labors."

They set him to digging at the end of the gully, into a wall of dried mud as hard as stone. All he had to work with was the steel bar he used to change flat tires. Tom stood motionless at his back, his arms folded across the chest of his messy shirt, while Davey patrolled the area, occasionally firing a round at a rock that caught his fancy. Carl didn't know where Cessy was. She had said something about being hungry and wandered off into the bush. She hadn't said a thing when Davey knocked the wind out of him. The bitch.

"I can't imagine what I did to offend you," he remarked to Tom as Davey moved out of earshot.

"I bet," Tom said.

"You're crazy if you think these people aren't going to screw you over when they're done with me."

"Shut up."

"No, I want to talk," Carl said, using the metal bar as a lever and knocking out a chunk of dirt. He was surprised to see the missing lump create a small hole in the wall. He peered inside; he could have been peering into the abyss beyond the farthest star. "Is this Valta?"

"I don't know."

"You betray a friend for something you don't know a thing about?"

"Shut up."

"All right. Whatever you say, Tom."

"We're not friends."

Carl turned. The three-quarter moon had risen now and was hanging to the right of Tom's head. Carl weighed the bar in his hand. Davey was heading farther away, rounding the curve of a bluff, probably searching out a rabbit to murder. Tom stood defenseless.

"We've known each other a long time," Carl said, taking a step toward him. "Tell me what's going on?"

"You'll see."

"How did you get so strong?"

"Keep digging."

"Was the scavenger hunt a farce to get me out here?" He took another step, tightening his hold on the bar. "Why the thing with the clothes?"

A peculiar look touched Tom's flat features, sorrow mixed with uncertainty. He raised his right arm, studying the material of the bloody wool shirt as if he were seeing it for the first time.

"I gave you my clothes to wear," he said softly.

Carl felt his grip on the bar loosen. He couldn't strike Tom, no matter what he was trying to do to him. Carl recognized Tom's shirt.

It had belonged to Joe.

Carl returned to digging.

The moon had climbed high enough to clear the neighboring hills before Carl managed to chisel away enough of the wall that a person could pass through to the inside. Cessy had returned by then. She was in good spirits. She had found a pet, a starving stray dog with two rows of protruding ribs that needed maybe one more missed meal to burst through a mangled brown hide. Cessy was feeding him something dark and juicy from her hands that Carl decided would not benefit from a closer inspection.

"Are we ready?" she asked.

"Yes," Davey said, flipping on the flashlight and resting the rifle over his shoulder. "I'll lead. You follow me, Carl. Cessy and Tom will be at your back. Cessy, leave the dog out here."

"No," she said, patting the pooch on the head while it hungrily licked the palm of her other hand for the last remaining morsel of whatever she had been feeding it. "I like him."

"If you like him, leave him," Davey said, annoyed.

"No," she repeated, turning to Carl. "What should we name him?"

"Name him after me," he replied bitterly. "That way you'll have something to remember me by."

Cessy smiled. She approved.

They went inside.

Valta. Strange name for a mine, Rick had said. Then Davey had told Rick its history, no doubt giving him less than a tenth of what he really knew, and lying about that. The entrance was narrow. For the first quarter-mile they walked slow and hunched over, brushing the walls and ceiling with their arms and heads, knocking free what looked like fresh brown dirt. Then the way abruptly widened and they were able to stand up straight. It was only then that Carl could see they were in no ordinary mine.

There were no supporting wooden posts, and there was no need for them. The walls were no longer loose gravel, but hard black stone, folded in smooth rippled waves like cooled lava. An unnaturally flat floor stretched out before them. Hands of intelligence had labored here, but Carl doubted if they had been those of a century-old band of ill-equipped miners. Modern machinery probably couldn't have cut such a floor so deep in the ground, at any cost.

But what impressed Carl the most was the power of

the place, the sense of history. He could feel the weight of time bearing down on him, time that had seen far more bad than good. Many horrors, he knew, had occurred in these depths. He could feel the evil residue upon his skin as clearly as he would have felt the claws of a lizard crawling up his bare leg.

The others remained silent. Carl might have let loose with a witty sarcasm had he not been afraid Davey would give him another butt in the gut. Breathing was still a task. Davey gestured for them to continue forward, the beam of his flashlight revealing no end to the tunnel.

So they walked on, the ground sloping down and the air becoming thicker and fouler. The smell was no stranger to Carl. It was the same smell he'd encountered at the abandoned purple house, where Cessy's other pet had hung out. The tunnel began to twist and turn, branching into numerous narrow passageways. Yet Davey held to the main branch, quickening his pace the deeper they went. Only the dog protested the rigorous march. And Cessy quietly hushed him whenever he complained. Carl could only look back on the day and himself with disgust. Since he had bolted upright in bed that morning, he had been like a dog tied to Cessy's ankle.

"Hi, Carl, did I wake you?"

He would not have been surprised to learn she had known what he had been dreaming about. Carl guessed that they must be walking beneath the very spot where Joe had died.

Still, he did not understand.

At approximately two miles from the entrance,

perhaps half a mile beneath the surface, the tunnel came to an abrupt halt, opening into a wide circular chamber. Here Davey's flashlight had to strain to define their surroundings. The ceiling was domed, an incredible curve of hollowed-out stone, and the walls were similar to those of the tunnel they had just left, only these were smoother and contained thousands of quartz crystals, which glittered like a galaxy of stars when Davey passed the beam over them. Yet the dome was utterly black and featureless.

An empty sky.

At the far end of the chamber stood a triangular slab of stone, its apex pointed toward the tunnel, a shiny gray platform raised roughly three feet off the floor, thirty feet across at its base, where it blended in and merged with the wall. At the center of the base stood an arched doorway approximately eight feet high. Davey shone his light on it and Carl saw only darkness beyond. The intensity of the smell was debilitating. They had finally reached the source.

"So this is Valta," Carl said, more to hear the sound of his own voice. The tense despair of the chamber was heart-rending. Living beings had been tortured here, he was sure of it.

"A place without a beginning," Davey agreed. "Without an end."

"Your hidden waters stink," Carl remarked, half expecting Davey to belt him. But all Davey did was turn and smile.

"We have more digging for you to do," he said.

"I don't suppose it'll be for gold?"

"For the past." Davey gestured to the ground in

front of the triangular slab. "It's not as hard as it looks."

Carl still had the bar from his truck with him. Davey made him bring it. But Carl didn't think for an instant of clubbing Davey with it. He could have been holding a loaded rifle and still been defenseless against these creatures.

"I don't know," Carl said. "I don't want to mess my clothes."

Davey swung down the rifle and ran his hand along the barrel. "If I splattered your brains over your clothes, that would be a mess."

"But then your game would have all been wasted," Carl said. "You could have killed me in my bedroom this morning."

Davey thought that was funny and laughed. Tom came up at Carl's side and pushed him forward. "Dig," he snapped.

Carl took a step toward the triangular slab, glancing back at Cessy, who was down on her knees, patting the dog's head. She had dust in her long, curly black hair, and her white summer dress had been torn at the shoulder, revealing the upper portion of her tan right breast. She looked better for the wear. She looked absolutely ravishing. Her dark-blue eyes glittered like the crystals embedded in the walls.

"I told you," she said.

"I guess you did," he said. "Are you having fun?"

She hugged her dog. "Always."

It had finally become intolerable. Let them do what they wanted. Carl threw down the bar and spoke to them all. "I won't do it."

Tom took a step toward him and Carl braced himself for a hard blow. Davey quickly intervened, nodding in the direction of the tunnel.

"It doesn't matter," Davey said. "It'll be dug up."

Cessy leapt to her feet, disquiet darkening her carefree brow. "Who is it?" she demanded.

Davey smiled. "More victims."

CHAPTER
X

THEY ALMOST MISSED THE SIGN. TRACIE WAS FIFTY YARDS past it before Rick called it to her attention. She didn't bother to turn around. Shifting into reverse, she raced the Camaro backward, the dust sweeping over her windshield. She parked beside the post and jumped out, leaving the engine running. The cardboard box was empty. She inspected the wrong-turn sign and the you-should-know-by-now clue. The item listed on the typed page said, "one lost shirt." The tracks of a truck led to the left, off the road. She got back in her car.

"What did it say?" Rick asked.

Tracie pointed to the slopes of the deserted hills to their north, now clearly visible beneath the rays of the rising moon. "It said go that way."

With the purple house far behind them, Tracie had finally shown Rick and Paula the articles she had taken from the table. Paula didn't think the clippings meant Mr. Partridge had committed the acts, but Rick's attitude had surprised Tracie. He immediately began to take the matter more seriously, probably because they were now discussing specific crimes and not vague diabolical plots. He wanted to go straight to the police, which would have been fine with Tracie if it hadn't meant an hour of backtracking. Her heart warned her there wasn't much time. Already Carl and the others must have reached the last place on the list.

Tracie kept silent about what she had seen and heard inside the house. But she had begun to doubt if she was doing her friends a favor. She feared they would see worse before the night was over.

The path proved far rougher than the dirt road. She was ruining her car, but she didn't care. Carl's truck had left clear tracks in the baked earth. At least they knew they were on the right trail. Plus Paula felt they were approaching the area where Joe had died.

Tracie hadn't said any more about Joe, and Paula wasn't asking. It wasn't something they could talk about and pretend the universe hadn't suddenly adopted a new set of natural laws.

The path came to an end at the edge of a narrow ravine. Farther east it appeared wider and deeper. Carl's truck sat there silent and empty. Tracie got out and studied the vehicle. The engine was still cooling. They were not far behind. She had no illusions about where the others had gone. It didn't take a sharp eye to spot the opening in the side of the hill where the gully ended.

"I hope that's not the place we read about," Paula said from her place in the backseat behind Rick. Tracie leaned across Rick and pulled the flashlight out of the glove compartment. Rick had adjusted the coiled contact wire inside and it was working better.

"I'm going to check it out," Tracie said. "You two wait here."

"You're kidding," Rick said.

"I'm serious," Tracie said. "In fact, Paula, take my car and get out of here. Carl can give me a ride home."

"You can't go in there alone," Paula said.

"And you can't leave Rick out here alone," Tracie said. "Don't argue with me." She stepped back. "I'm going."

Paula got out of the car in a hurry, grabbing Tracie before she could take half a dozen steps toward the mine entrance.

"You know what that dude said about this place!" Paula said.

"But Carl's in there," Tracie said.

"Fine," Paula said. "Let's just wait here until Carl comes out of there."

Tracie shook her off. "I can't wait. He might not come out."

"Ladies," Rick said, "there's only one thing to do. Let me go."

"No," Paula said, shaking her head. "Absolutely not."

"You can't get your chair in there," Tracie said.

"Then why did Davey invite me here?" Rick said. "You said it yourself, Tracie. He directed the story about Valta at me. There must be room for me. Give me the flashlight. I'll see about Carl."

Tracie came and knelt by his side. He was clearly exhausted. He usually had a nap in the afternoon, and always went to bed early. She took his hand, the frailness of his return grip surprising even her.

"You're right," she said. "Davey did want you here,

maybe more than the rest of us. But that's why you must leave here. Davey has never liked you, Rick. He could hurt you."

Rick stared her in the eye, his face thin but his voice clear. "I'm beginning to believe you. A genuine scavenger hunt would never have brought us out this far. Valta might exist. The diary we read could be accurate. That's scary. It scares me as much as it scares you. But it's exciting, too. I don't have a lot of excitement in my life. I read books, I go to the library, I go to the doctors and I—I wait for something to change for me." Rick took a breath and glanced at the dark opening. "I *have* to go in there."

Tracie lowered her head. They were fools, she thought, to take the bait. But maybe it was meant to be this way. They would all go inside. But she already knew they would not all be coming out.

CHAPTER
XI

CARL FELT SICK WITH GUILT WHEN HE REALIZED WHO had arrived. Tracie had found his watch. He could see it on her wrist. He could see her death in the glint in Davey's eyes. Dropping to his knees, knowing it would be a wasted try, Carl grabbed the steel bar and swung it toward Davey's head. Carl didn't even see him duck. Davey simply was no longer there. And then Carl was lying dazed on the black ground. Davey had caught him on the side of the head this time, bringing stars to his eyes and a trickle of blood over his cheek. Rolling onto his side, Carl sat up weakly, telling himself there had to be a way to stop them, while simultaneously asking himself why there had to be a way. For all he knew, an atomic bomb might not have slowed them.

Tracie led the way, a flashlight in her hand, Paula and Rick not far behind. They were filthy with dust. Hauling Rick and his wheelchair through the initial passageway must have been a struggle. Rick's eyes were all over the chamber, filled with awe. Paula had a firm hand on his shoulder, her face grave. Fifty feet out, Tracie signaled for her companions to halt. She stepped forward alone.

"Leave him alone, Mr. Senior-Class President," she called. "We have the police, and they're not far behind."

Davey strode casually toward her, his smile cocky and arrogant, his hold on the rifle loose. He carried it for pleasure, Carl knew, rather than any practical reason. He liked playing the boss. Carl glanced at Cessy. She was no longer petting her dog. The arrival of the others had caught her off guard. Tom stood on the triangular slab, not far from the arched doorway, as motionless as a statue.

"Tracie," Davey said. "What a pleasure."

"Carl," she called. "Are you all right?"

"I'm fine." He stood slowly, a burning pain between his ears to match the pain in his abdomen.

"We don't want any trouble," Tracie told Davey. "We'll leave with Carl and that can be the end of it."

"It took you all day to get there," Davey said. "What's the rush?"

Tracie glared at him. "We know about *you.*"

"Tracie," Carl said. "Don't worry about me. Get out of here."

"Did you go to the house?" Davey asked, enjoying himself. "Did you read what I've been up to?"

"What is this?" Cessy asked.

Davey glanced at his sister. "It's no concern of yours."

"Your brother's been cutting up people with razor blades," Tracie told her. "What do you think of that?"

"I see," Cessy replied, not overly impressed. "How did you come to be here?"

"Your brother planted another set of clues," Tracie said.

Cessy knelt down and caressed her pet, losing interest in the subject. "None of this is necessary," she muttered.

"It is necessary!" Davey snapped, his anger erupting out of nowhere. But he quickly regained his jovial continence and turned back to Tracie. He nodded at her flashlight. "That isn't exactly a high-caliber weapon you're carrying."

"The police," she began.

"The police!" he interrupted with a snort. "There are no police." He looked past Tracie. "Hello, Rick. How are you?"

"I'm fine, thanks. Tell me more about this place?"

Davey chuckled. "Master Richard, you're going to learn all about it first hand." He moved to step past Tracie. She shot out a hand to stop him.

"Don't you dare," she swore.

Davey slowly lifted her hand off his shoulder. "I don't dare, my dear. I just do it."

"Davey," Tom said. "They shouldn't be here."

"What?"

"This is not what we discussed," Tom said.

Davey paused, thinking, and then nodded. "You're right, we should get back to business. I'm glad you reminded me." He stared at Tom, catching his eye. "There are some materials I left in the truck. I'll need them to make your transfer with Carl. Could you get them for me?"

Transfer?

Carl didn't much like the sound of that word.

"What materials?" Tom asked.

Davey continued to stare at Tom, his eyes unblinking. His voice took on a much softer tone. Carl wasn't sure if he heard it with his ears, or inside his head.

"They're in the truck," Davey said. "You'll see them. Get them for me now."

"All right," Tom said, taking a step off the slab, then halting, shaking himself slightly.

He's hypnotizing him.

"Now," Davey repeated.

"Where?" Tom asked, frowning.

"The truck," Davey seemed to whisper. "Go there."

Tom glanced at Cessy. She didn't look up. She seemed to be thinking, too. Tom's eyes went back to Davey, whose gaze never left Tom's face. For several seconds nothing happened. Then Tom began to walk stiffly toward the tunnel. Yet he paused as he passed Paula. Her eyes were wide. She removed her hand from Rick's shoulder and stretched it out hesitantly in his direction before letting it fall weakly at her side.

"Who are you?" she asked, and her voice trembled.

Tracie shifted her light in their direction and Carl could see a ripple of confusion spread across Tom's ordinarily blank expression. He was on the verge of speaking when Davey reinforced his order.

"Hurry, Tom," Davey said.

Tom left. Two miles of pure black lay before him and he didn't even bring a flashlight with him. Carl realized that Tracie must have made the same observation. She paled as Davey returned his attention to her. The play of their opposing lights was hard on the eyes. The walls crawled with elongated shadows.

"I want you two to help Carl dig," Davey said to the girls.

"Go to hell," Paula sneered.

Davey moved toward her. No, he took a step in her direction and then he was at Paula's side, gripping the big finger on her right hand and pulling her slowly and painfully into the air. Incredibly, in the blur of motion, he had also managed to slip his flashlight into his belt. Tracie whirled, obviously shaken by how he had gotten past her.

"There are many hells in this universe," Davey told Paula. "Which should we visit first?"

Paula's mouth dropped open. Then she pressed her lips together and spat in his face. It was a valiant gesture, and foolhardy. Davey flicked his wrist. The crack of the snapping bone in her finger was heard by all. Paula screamed. Davey clamped his hand over her mouth with the same hand that was holding the rifle.

"Are you sorry for what you just did?" he asked.

Paula nodded vigorously.

Davey released her and she crumpled to the ground, grabbing her hand and doubling up. He wiped the spit from his face. "You are going to be even more sorry," he said.

"Davey," Rick spoke up, trying to sound casual but clearly shaken by what he had just witnessed. "You and I have to talk. Intimidation is not the way to handle this. You obviously have a lot more to you than meets the eye."

Davey smiled. "You think so?"

"Oh, yeah," Rick said, a worried eye cast toward his sister, who had yet to get up. Carl could see she was in a lot of pain. "You must be connected with the amazing people who built this place. I'd like to hear all about it. We could write a book together on the subject. You'd be famous."

"I have been famous in your history," Davey said, throwing Cessy a look. "Many books have been written about me. Many stories have been told."

"That's great," Rick said. "So why don't we all sit down and have a nice talk and let things cool down?"

"Cool down?" Davey asked. He let his head fall back and looked up at the black dome, drinking in the obnoxious fumes as if they were a draft of scented air. "No, I'm having too much fun to cool down." He glanced down at Paula, who was trying to crawl on her knees. For a moment he seemed to contemplate kicking her and breaking a couple of her ribs for good measure. But then he spoke to Tracie, who stood helpless nearby. "I'll let your friend sit out this little exercise," he said. "But you help Carl dig. We have to finish with the scavenger hunt."

Tracie gave in, her tough stance in ruins, obviously realizing that Davey was a far more powerful adversary than they could have imagined. Davey handed her a hunting knife. He must have taken an extra one from the box beneath the drain cover on the track. For Carl, that seemed a lifetime ago. The knife was for digging. Carl picked up the bar. Davey directed them to the area at the tip of the triangular slab. He made them go down on their knees. The stance appealed to him. Yet he did not sit to watch them work. He went off to confer with Cessy, who seemed to neither approve nor disapprove of his tactics. She didn't need the entertainment, Carl thought. She had her dog to amuse her.

"Your head is bleeding," Tracie whispered.

Carl glanced over his shoulder. Paula was still doubled up in pain. He could sympathize. "I'm fine. How did you get here?"

"We followed your tracks," she said. "It's a long story. Do you know this is close to the place Joe died?"

"Yes."

"What does it mean?"

"I don't know," he said.

"But who are these people? How can Davey move so fast and be so strong?"

"I don't know," he repeated.

"Are they human?"

He glanced at her. She had set the flashlight on the slab to keep her hands free. The focus of the beam caught her below the waist, sending harsh shadows over her face. Yet there was something in her eyes that seemed to resist the gloom of the chamber, a trace of the sunshine he always used to imagine she carried with her. He would have given his life to know she was far away, and safe.

Or so he told himself.

"No," he said. "They can't be human."

"What are they going to do to us?"

She was asking him for hope. It was the least he could give her for his cowardly mistake of leaving the watch. But all he had to offer her was a lie. "They would have killed us already if that was all they wanted," he said.

"Yeah."

"Tracie? You said something about knowing of crimes Davey had committed?"

"I broke into the purple house. There was a collection of articles inside on ghastly murders. I'm sure he killed all those poor people."

"Then why did you follow us here?" he asked.

"To rescue you."

"What?"

She tried to force a smile, but didn't quite make it, lowering her head instead. She was too smart to fall for his lie. Her eyes moistened. "I had to come, Carl."

Davey had remarked that the ground was not as hard as it looked, and in the place where he set them to work, that was definitely true. In fact, the earth appeared to have been recently uncovered, and then replaced. Besides being soft, it was uneven. They set aside their tools after a couple of minutes and just used their hands. The soil had a grainy texture to it, and was somewhat sticky. It was not long before they had built up respectable piles to either side of the point of the slab.

Four feet down, Tracie's hand struck an object. A note of surprise passed her lips and Davey immediately scurried over. Cessy stood and followed at a more leisurely pace, the dog at her heels. By this time, Paula was sitting up and breathing normally, although it was clear her finger needed medical attention. Davey waved Paula and Rick over with the barrel of the rifle. They approached reluctantly, and as a group they gathered around the hole.

"Do any of you know what's buried here?" Davey asked.

"If we guess correctly," Rick asked, "do we still get a free trip to Hawaii?"

"You'll get something far more valuable than that," Davey said.

"What?" Rick asked.

"Your freedom," Davey said.

"You'll let us go?" Tracie asked.

"I promise," Davey said.

"I don't believe you," Tracie said.

"You should," Davey said.

"Why should we?" Tracie asked.

"You don't have any choice," Davey said.

Cessy moved to Tracie's side. Cessy had changed since entering the chamber. She was more serious, and there was a vibe about her that Carl could only describe as powerful.

"You guess," Cessy said to Tracie.

Tracie hesitated. "A body."

"Close," Davey said. "But you must be more specific. I'll give you one more chance."

Tracie glanced at Paula, perspiration breaking out on her forehead. "You're just playing with us," she said to Davey.

"You won't know for sure unless you try," Davey said.

"You'll let us all go?"

"I might," Davey said.

"You have to swear it," Tracie said.

Davey shrugged. "I swear it."

Tracie glanced up at the black dome, back down at the black hole in the ground. "Joe's body," she whispered.

"Close," Davey said.

"Am I right?" Tracie demanded.

Davey smiled. "There's much more to it than that. And one might also say, much less."

"Are you two Daniel and Claire Stevens?" Tracie asked.

"I see you've been doing your homework," Davey said.

"Who?" Carl asked.

"Two of the people who *supposedly* were there, but they died in this gold mine a hundred years ago," Tracie said.

"I thought there were four people?" Carl asked, trying to recall the details of the story.

"Only two died," Tracie said. She gestured to Cessy and Davey. "These two survived."

Davey did not respond to the comment, but strolled to the base of the slab. Laying the rifle aside beside the arched doorway, he twisted his neck around the curve of the stone wall and his head disappeared. It did not simply become difficult to see in the blackness beyond; it *became* a part of the blackness. But then he pulled back and his head was where it had always been. The act appeared to have invigorated him. He strode toward them again, leaving the rifle behind.

"You were asking?" he said.

"Davey," Cessy said.

"Let me talk!" he snapped. "You've talked all day!"

Cessy shrugged, falling silent. Tracie took a step forward.

"Was I right?" she insisted. "Are you going to let us go?"

Davey waved his hand. "Those are such boring questions. Are there no others?"

"Yes," Rick spoke up, wheeling his chair closer to the slab. Tracie gave him a look of pure exasperation, but didn't stop him. The horror of the chamber had not dimmed his curiosity. "Tell us about this place and the people who built it?" he asked again.

"They were very old," Davey said. "And they were not people as you know people. They were of a higher order."

"How old?" Rick asked.

"Hundreds of millions of years."

"That's impossible," Rick began. "Man has only been on this planet—"

"Man!" Davey interrupted loudly. "Man is nothing! Man is a soft-skinned freak! He will have his day and then he will be gone! We ruled this planet for millions of years and we will rule it again!"

His words echoed throughout the chamber, resonating with the walls. Carl noticed then that there was a pattern to the arrangement of the many crystals. He wondered if they didn't form a written language of some kind.

"A metal grave for terrible lizards," Rick muttered. He shook his head. "It's not possible."

"It's your history," Davey said. "It's your future."

"What is it?" Tracie asked. Rick looked up at her.

"The dinosaurs ruled the earth for millions of years," he said. "He's implying that an intelligent reptilian race evolved out of them and went on to form a civilization. Is that correct, Davey?"

Davey nodded, watching his sister, who was watching him.

"Gimme a break," Paula muttered. Carl could hardly believe her nerve. She pulled out a cigarette and went to light it with her uninjured hand, until Cessy raised a hand and caught Paula's eye in much the way Davey had caught Tom's before he had sent him away on his errand. Paula quickly put away her lighter.

"How far advanced were they?" Rick asked. "Did they have computers? Could they travel in space?"

Davey chuckled. "They had more important things to do with their time. The secrets they unlocked make your science seem like child's play."

"How do you know this?" Tracie asked.

"I know," Davey said.

"What were the secrets?" Rick asked.

Davey stared down at the hole they had dug. "The secrets of cause and effect," he said, his tone softening, changing, taking on a faint hissing sound. "Of life and death. They learned how to balance the scales in their favor. To break the scales, even, and turn them around." He pointed to the ground. "Finish digging."

"No," Tracie said. "You told us you would let us go if I guessed correctly."

"Did I say that?"

"You know damn well you did," Tracie said.

Davey smiled. "And you know damn well what a liar I am." He gestured to the ground once more, this time indicating Carl should dig alone. "You should probably be the one to finish this. Dig."

Carl got back down on his knees, searching for the spot that had caused Tracie to stop, having the awful thought that what he was feeling for might be waiting to bite his fingers off. Yet when he first touched it, the thing seemed innocent enough. He brushed aside another layer of the earth. It was only a pair of sunglasses.

His relief lasted a grand total of two seconds.

Someone was wearing the glasses.

Davey laughed aloud as Carl let out a cry and jerked his hand back and leapt to his feet. Stepping into the hole, Davey used the tip of his boot to expose the face of the unfortunate soul. After all they had witnessed, it shouldn't have been a shock, and yet the sight of the corpse almost caused Carl to faint.

It was Mr. Partridge.

"I told him to bury himself at least half a dozen feet under," Davey said and sighed. "Good help is so hard to find these days."

"What—what's he doing here?" Rick asked, stuttering.

"Why, he's the grand prize," Davey said. "Paula, dear, weren't you in one of Mr. Partridge's classes?"

"Yes, and he reminded me of you," Paula said. "He bored me to tears."

"To tears?" Davey asked, holding her gaze a moment. Paula tried to meet it, but ended up looking down. Davey went on. "He might have been a bit dull at times, but you see he was only a puppet. Being senior-class president and having so many other responsibilities, I couldn't always keep his strings uncrossed."

"What's that mean?" Carl asked.

"He was my alter ego," Davey said.

"You ran the club?" Carl asked.

"Naturally," Davey said.

"Is he dead?" Rick asked.

"Sure," Davey said.

"Was he ever alive?" Tracie asked.

"A more profound question with no easy answer," Davey replied, leaning over. "But we could say that a piece of him must have been alive at one time. Look at this."

Davey removed Mr. Partridge's sunglasses.

Empty sockets stared out from behind them.

Tracie grimaced. "What happened to his eyes?"

"Oh, he hasn't had any eyes for a year now," Davey said, putting the sunglasses on himself. He waited for them to respond. "It was a year ago today, when the clouds above were dark and heavy and the stars above them had come into a favorable aspect. I told you, Tracie, you were close. But, as they say, close only counts in horseshoes and grenades. Don't any of you understand?" Davey sighed and crouched down beside the figure. "Perhaps this will help. Let me show you something."

"No," Paula said, ready to be sick.

"But I insist," Davey said, tugging on the pale flaccid flesh of Mr. Partridge's left cheek. "You've all been dying to know what's going on. It wouldn't be fair for me to keep you in suspense forever."

Carl's stomach heaved as Davey began to rip Mr. Partridge's facial skin off. Davey did it effortlessly, in handfuls, and yet, when he was through, there was no blood. There was only a pile of imitation flesh a special effects man might have had in his supplies, and a hollow white skull that could have sat unprotected in the desert sand for over a year beneath a boiling sun.

"You will recognize the teeth, Paula," Davey said, standing back. "The bottom row is crooked. I suppose he didn't have the money for braces. A shame, don't you think? He would have been a more handsome sight with a little dental work. Not that you cared. You must have kissed this mouth a hundred times and enjoyed every minute of it."

Paula could not speak. She could not move. Nor could Carl. *He* recognized the teeth. Only Tracie had the will left to say it.

"This is Joe's skeleton," she whispered.

Davey clapped his hands together. "You, I definitely must send to Hawaii! Yes, this is Joe. He's the one who made the scavenger hunt possible. Too bad we don't have Tom here to tell you all about it. The plan was for you to dig up Joe and then have Tom put on his sunglasses. The gesture would have been so symbolic. It's a shame I had to send him away." Davey took off the glasses and gave them a brief inspection. "You must recognize these, Carl?"

"They belonged to Joe," he heard himself say. All the clothes they had found, all the clothes Tom was now wearing, had been Joe's.

Except for the gold chain. Joe had given that to Paula the night before they had gone into the desert.

Davey nodded. "The flood washed him down here. I know Master Richard will say that's impossible, but after all, he's not as smart as he thinks or he wouldn't be here. In this place, anything goes. It wouldn't be incorrect to say this place sent the flood to fetch Joe. We have a habit of getting whatever we need."

"We?" Tracie said.

"The terrible lizards," Davey said, and gestured to the skeleton. "This guy washed down here and through this door and lost his skin as well as his clothes. But in doing so, he gave us a chance to come back out and play. We made a deal with him, a deal I might say we have so far honored to the letter. We were the ones who put his bones back outside so that he could be found and have a decent funeral. I must confess, though, that we had a selfish motive. We didn't want people continuing to search this area. They might have found our special door before we were ready for them."

"But we buried Joe," Tracie said.

"No," Davey said. "You buried the cemetery's fat security guard. Cessy and I stopped by the night before the funeral and collected Joe. Even back then, we were thinking of having a scavenger hunt, and we wanted to have a special 'one of a kind item' for the last stop on the list." Davey nodded. "You should have been there. The guard caught us in the act. We had a time putting him in Joe's coffin. He put up a wonderful fight. He thought we were going to kill him, when all we did was gag and bind him." Davey shook his head. "It's amazing the pall bearers didn't notice the extra weight."

"What did you mean when you said you've come back out to play?" Rick asked.

Davey studied Paula and Tracie. "The girls know what I mean," he said. "Carl knows, too, although he's too ashamed to admit his role in this whole affair."

"I have nothing to do with this," Carl said bitterly.

"I've heard different," Davey said.

"But who was Mr. Partridge?" Tracie asked.

"I told you," Davey said. "He was a puppet—a pile of skin and bones who responded to my will. I *made* him. But I wouldn't worry about him. You have other things to worry about."

"How are you connected with the ancient race?" Rick asked.

Davey stopped. "I'm one of them."

"You're millions of years old?" Rick asked, doubtful.

"I'm immortal," Davey bragged.

"But obviously the same couldn't be said for the rest of your race," Rick said, probably not intending to taunt him but doing so nevertheless. Davey showed definite signs of undergoing another one of his volatile mood swings, but Rick continued on unaware. "The dinosaurs disappeared overnight. Certain dinosaurs have even been found fossilized in midstride. Some scientists have theorized that the earth may have been hit with a huge meteorite that instantly changed the climate. If you are from a race that was alive at that time, then you must have some idea what happened?"

Davey's emotional explosion was averted by Cessy. Taking a step in front of Rick, she turned her back on her brother, blocking Rick from Davey's line of vision.

"It wasn't a meteorite," she said. "It was nothing a human being could understand."

"Was there a war?" Rick asked.

Cessy hesitated. "Not exactly."

Davey stepped down from the slab and stood near Rick's chair. He had not appreciated the interruption. "I'm getting tired of these fool questions," he said. "A demonstration is what we need."

Cessy regarded him impatiently. "Tom isn't here."

"Our debts should be satisfied first," Davey said. "Our time runs short."

"That wasn't in our plan," Cessy said.

"I'm changing the plan."

"Is that why these others are here?"

"Yes."

"You've talked too much," Cessy said. "You've wasted the purpose of the scavenger hunt. You've lost your tension."

"Tension?" Davey asked, surprised. "How could that be lost?"

"You fool," Cessy said.

Davey backed off a step, his stare fixed hard upon her face. Then he moved. Carl's eyes couldn't follow exactly *how* he did it, but they caught enough to know *what* he did. He grabbed Cessy's dog and flung it toward the arched doorway. Cessy reacted almost as quickly, but she was a step behind. The animal's tail slipped through her fingers. It went beyond her reach, beyond the door, and was gone.

Cessy closed her eyes and rested her head against the stone wall, her fist clenched.

The screams began.

Carl had heard many wounded animals in his day and had always been deeply affected. Yet nothing had prepared him for the sounds Cessy's dog made as it died. Besides the pitiful yelps, he heard wild splashing noises and a faint though distinct sizzling sound, as if the animal had landed in a reservoir of highly corrosive acid.

And, he knew, one of them was going to be next.

The yelps finally ceased, but the silence that followed brought no relief.

"You were saying something about tension?" Davey said to his sister. Cessy slowly lifted her head off the wall and opened her eyes, staring at her brother. Carl hoped to see anger, sorrow at least, and was disappointed on both counts. Cessy looked cool as ever.

"This is your place," she told her brother.

"That's right," Davey said. "Cheer up. You'll get another pet out of it, one more to your liking."

"I prefer to choose my own pets," Cessy said.

"Do you have a choice in who you kiss?" Paula asked her. Carl did not understand the reference, although Davey seemed to. He strode toward Paula and stood hovering over her.

"I don't like you," Davey said.

Paula began to snap at him, then glanced at the black doorway and lowered her head. "That's all right," she muttered.

"What?" Davey asked.

"I said, that's all right."

"For whom?" Davey said.

Paula raised her head and swallowed. "For both of us."

"What about for your brother?" Davey asked. Paula didn't say anything. Davey smiled. "Untie his shoelaces."

"Huh?" Paula said.

"I said, untie his shoelaces."

"Why?" Paula asked, trembling.

"I can untie them myself," Rick said, bending over. Davey stopped him with a hand on the shoulder.

"No, I want your sister to do it," he said. "I want her to remove your shoelaces and bind your ankles to your chair."

163

Paula shook her head faintly. "No."

"Davey," Tracie said, a tear falling over her cheek. "Don't."

"Now," Davey told Paula.

"Carl," Tracie moaned. "Do something."

"He has already done his part," Davey said. "That's why you're all here." His hand shot out and grabbed Paula by the hair and pushed her down by Rick's feet. "I have no patience for those I don't like," he snapped. "I won't hesitate to throw you in the water."

Paula began to undo the laces. With her broken finger and shaking hands, it took forever, and when it came to binding Rick's ankles to the chair, she simply couldn't or wouldn't do it. Rick ended up having to help her. Davey let him. Enough appeared to be going as Davey wished; he wasn't going to quibble with every point. Rick had to be the bravest kid alive. Rick had to know he was tying the noose on the rope that was going to hang him. Carl prayed to God for an end to the madness.

"He has already done his part."

But God did not answer. Perhaps he could not hear the prayers cried to him from a place as forsaken as this. Carl did not understand how Davey could blame him for his friend's predicament.

Tracie stepped to Davey's side, her hands out in a gesture of pleading. "You can't push him through that door," she said.

"I can," Davey said. "And I will."

"No! Please, Davey? Anything but that."

Davey smiled. "You say please to a monster? You can do better than that, Tracie."

She paused, lowering her hands, seeing that begging only made him worse. "What do you want?"

"To balance the scales," he said.

"What does that mean?" Tracie asked.

"To stay alive," he said, nodding to the doorway. "We need to sacrifice."

"To come back from the dead?" Tracie asked.

"To come back and play," Davey said. He pointed to a dark corner of the chamber. Something moved near the wall, something low and long, like the lizard Davey had crushed at the purple house. A new pet for Cessy. Carl thought it interesting how it had appeared immediately after the dog left the scene. Cessy continued to watch the proceedings with complete indifference.

"What does the sacrifice do?" Tracie asked. "Besides balance the scales?"

"It creates a tension that strains the fabric between this world and another." Again Davey indicated the doorway. "Here the fabric is already very thin. It is a special place. It is my place."

"Then you are from the past," Tracie said.

Davey shrugged. "You mentioned the dead. They don't keep time. You can think of it any way you wish." He paused again. "Our tension diminishes. Are you snug and secure in your seat, Rick?"

"I really think we could talk this over," Rick said.

"Can you swim?" Davey asked.

"No," Rick said.

"It's never too late to learn," Davey said, taking a step toward him. Paula leapt up and blocked the path. Tracie touched Davey's arm.

"I have an offer for you," Tracie said.

Davey was interested. "Yes?"

"Does it matter who you use to balance the scales?"

Davey glanced at Carl. "It can."

"But does it matter in this case?" Tracie asked.

Davey patted Rick fondly on top of the head. "This young man has already prequalified himself with his many unkind remarks toward me."

"I was only kidding," Rick said. Paula stepped back and wrapped her arms over his shoulders, beginning to cry.

"Use me," Tracie said.

Davey considered. "An interesting offer. Do you have any conditions?"

"Yes," Tracie said. "You have to let the others go."

"I have to give you my *word?*" Davey asked.

"Yes," Tracie said.

"Didn't we go through this a few minutes ago?" Davey asked.

"If I can give you what you need," Tracie said, "you should have no reason not to let the others go."

"That's logical," Davey said. "You're a brave girl. I'll make you a counteroffer. I'll spare Rick if you'll choose another for me."

"What?" Tracie said.

"Choose between Paula and Carl," Davey said. "You have twenty seconds to decide."

"But?" Tracie began.

"You now have eighteen seconds," Davey said.

Tracie stopped dumb. Carl wanted to help her. He wanted to tell her to choose him. But he couldn't get the screams of the dog out of his head. He was a coward. Could that be what Davey had been referring to a minute ago? When the flood of water had come down upon them in the gully, Joe had called to him for help, and he had tried to help him. . . .

After thinking about it for a few seconds.

He had almost forgotten about that. The delay. The hesitation.

The creature near the far wall slithered in the black earth.

"I'll go in place of my brother," Paula said.

"No," Rick said. "This guy's a lizard. He won't keep his word."

"Twelve seconds," Davey said.

"I said, I'll be your sacrifice," Paula said.

"But *I* said, Tracie is to decide," Davey said.

"I can't," Tracie whispered. "Carl?"

"You want me to use Carl?" Davey asked.

"No."

"Paula then?"

"No! I told you I'd go!"

"You have five seconds," Davey said.

The five seconds went by. It didn't take long. Davey shook his head sadly and put a hand on the back of Rick's wheelchair. Paula tried to stop him, but he pushed her gently away. Gently for him. Paula ended up on her butt on the black ground to the right of the slab. Davey did not want to knock her out. Davey wanted her to watch. He needed his tension. Paula scampered to her feet, but was stopped this time by Tracie, who must have decided it was hopeless to resist. Davey nodded his approval.

"Would all human beings step down from the altar," he said. "Carl, if you would please?"

Carl stood slightly forward and to the left of the

doorway. The rifle was where Davey had left it—leaning against the wall to the right of the doorway. Carl figured his chances of reaching it in time to get off a shot at Davey's head were close to zero. But he was through hesitating.

He leapt for the rifle.

Then he was flying through the air. But not in the direction of the rifle. Davey had struck him again, hard on the side. He was flying toward the black doorway.

He missed it by a foot, hitting the upper left side of the archway, and fell toward the floor. Yet, even as he fell, he retained a large portion of his forward momentum. Landing, he skidded over the end of the gray slab, and almost off the edge of the world.

An instinct in his left hand saved him. When he came to his senses, he was hanging over the side of the precipice, his feet dangling below into a place where they could not be found, the three middle fingers of his left hand all that lay between him and a bath that would ruin his smooth eighteen-year-old complexion for good. Cessy and Davey stepped to the edge of the doorway and peered down at him, looking more than ten feet tall.

They spoke. He saw their mouths move.

But he could not hear them.

Carl knew he should swing his right hand up and tighten his hold on the lower corner of the doorway, but was unable to communicate the message to his muscles. The fumes were overpowering. His brain was not working correctly, and it wasn't just because he was terrified. Something in the smell was finally getting to him. He was in a black void. His eyes could see that, which translated to mean they couldn't see anything. But behind his eyes, in his head, in that deep portion of the brain that scientists sometimes called the reptilian mind, because evolution had developed it first, millions of years before mammals were even a dream in the genetic code of a mutated DNA, he saw a different reality. He saw the past, or the future, or maybe death itself.

He saw the other side, where Cessy and Davey had come from.

His vision expanded, became unlocalized. Suddenly he could see in a multitude of directions at once. He realized there were many chambers beyond the doorway, each as large as an entire world, each lay one upon the other, and he understood what Davey had meant when he said there were many hells in the universe.

Each world was a horror.

But before he could look closer, the vision collapsed.

Carl's grip slipped a notch. He was back on the wrong side of the doorway. Davey was raising his boot. Cessy was shaking her head. Then Davey made a soundless laugh, and Cessy knelt down and Carl felt a grip ten times greater than his own take hold of his arm.

Then he was standing on his feet in the center of the slab.

"There aren't any bullets in the gun, Carl," Davey said.

Carl collapsed. Soft arms circled him. Tracie was pulling him off the slab. He was alive. He had come within inches of death and survived. Yet nothing had changed. The evil gods still demanded their sacrifice. Davey lifted Rick and his wheelchair onto the slab, both of Rick's legs tied securely to his footrest. Carl struggled to his feet.

"Cessy," he said. "You can stop him."

Davey looked to his sister. Cessy ignored both of them. She was studying Rick.

"I have never met another like you," she said.

"I'm a one-of-a-kind item," Rick said bravely.

Cessy glanced at Paula. She was not watching. She stood with her head bowed and her eyes tightly clenched. She was breathing strangely, and she wasn't crying. She might have been going into shock.

"Nothing changes," Cessy said.

"Only I know this secret," Davey told her.

Cessy turned her dark eyes on him. It would not have been correct to say their features were identical, not as far as some male/female twins went. Cessy's eyes were bigger, rounder. Yet they possessed, Carl saw finally, no more warmth than Davey's. As she regarded her brother, Carl glimpsed something truly terrible in them.

"Do what you will," she said finally.

"No," Carl cried.

They paid him no heed. The sacrifice would not be stopped. Tracie hugged Carl's side, and he wrapped an arm around her. He had never held Tracie before. He wished to God he had accepted her invitation to be a part of her team.

Davey spoke to Rick. "Say your farewells."

Rick turned their way. His cheeks were damp, but his voice came out even. "It's not so bad, guys, really. I was going to die anyway. It was an exciting day. I think it was the best day of my life." He paused. "I love you all." He glanced at his sister, who could not bear to look, to even hear, and whispered, "Love you, Paula. Bye."

Rick turned away so that they could not see his face, his wheelchair pointed in the direction of the arched doorway, Davey to his right, Cessy to his left. The chamber fell silent. Davey stretched out a hand and placed it on top of Rick's head. He began to whisper quietly, rapidly, his voice imitating the hiss of a snake. Yet, possibly because of his brief vision of the other side, Carl got the gist of what was being said. It was an invocation. Davey was calling upon unnatural forces. But he wasn't trying to balance the scales. He was trying to cheat them.

Rick became completely still. Carl prayed he was slipping into a trance where he wouldn't feel anything when he hit the searing water. It seemed a futile prayer. Davey's magic obviously relied upon pain.

Yet this time someone may have heard Carl's prayer.

Cessy stood idle during the proceedings, apparently uninterested in whether Rick died or if Davey succeeded in lengthening his weekend pass in the land of the living and warm-blooded. But at the exact instant Davey stopped chanting and placed his palm on Rick's back, Cessy looked up and stared Davey right in the eye.

"Tom's returned," she said.

"No," Davey said, distracted.

Cessy leaned closer. "Tom's returned," she repeated.

Davey glanced up at the entrance to the chamber, confused. He let go of Rick and took a step away from the doorway, toward the tip of the slab.

"I don't see him," he said.

"See him," Cessy commanded, her eyes focused on the back of his head. Then, suddenly, she reached down and took Rick's head in her hands. Her mouth twisted in an odd line, and the sound that passed her lips was similar to a word Davey had repeated several times in his invocation, only at a much higher pitch.

Then Cessy twisted Rick's head. Hard. She broke his neck, and Carl felt his own heart break with the sound of his young friend's bones.

Cessy shoved Rick through the doorway. Davey whirled around. There followed a loud splash, but no screams. Only blessed silence.

At least he had not suffered.

Tracie sagged against Carl's side, the strength leaving her limbs. Carl had to support her, quickly removing the flashlight from her hand lest it drop and leave them in the dark with these two murderers.

"It's done," Cessy told her brother.

"But I wanted to do it!" Davey complained, jumping to the door and peering inside. "I don't hear him."

"I do," Cessy said softly.

"What have you done?" Davey demanded.

"What could I do?" Cessy asked.

Davey fumed for a moment. Then he began to calm down. "I had completed the calling," he said finally, seeming to agree with her. It struck Carl then that Davey had not heard Cessy's brief chant, nor had he heard Rick's neck breaking.

Could Cessy have momentarily hypnotized him?

"It's good," Davey continued. "I remain strong. We must continue."

"With what?" Cessy asked.

"With Carl."

"Tom hasn't returned," she replied, a faint note of sarcasm entering her voice. She definitely had changed since coming into this place, even more so since Davey had killed her dog. The mysterious lizard continued to flop about the far corner. Davey shifted indecisively on his altar, probably trying to decide if he wanted to fry or boil his next victim.

Carl couldn't believe Rick was really gone. Even the boy's body must already be in ruins. The acid would first eat away . . .

It was better not to think about it.

"Why don't you do us all at once and get it over with?" Tracie cried, straightening herself by Carl's side.

Davey perked up at Tracie's outburst. He strode toward them, withdrawing a hunting knife from his back pocket.

"This is sharp," he said, holding it up so that they could examine the blade. It was not the same type of knife they had found at the beginning of the scavenger hunt. "You could skin a newlywed with a knife like this. I tell you that so you will be better able to understand the demonstration I am about to perform."

"What kind of demonstration?" Carl asked.

"It concerns you, Carl," Davey said. "Did you know you're not your everyday high school senior?"

"What do you mean?" he asked.

"Do you have nightmares, Carl?" Davey asked.

"Sometimes."

"What are they about?"

"I don't remember," he lied.

"Do you remember your best friend Joe?"

"Yes," Carl said.

"Where did he die?"

"Near here."

"How did he die?" Davey asked.

"You know. You said it already."

"Say it again for me, Carl."

"He drowned."

"In the desert?"

"Yes," Carl said.

"Did you try to save him? Before he drowned?"

"Yes."

"You risked your life?"

"Why do you want to know?" Carl asked, beginning to feel more uneasy, if possible.

"I want to know how close you came to risking your life. I also want to know how late you were in taking the risk."

"Why?" Carl asked.

"Because I think—and Tom agrees with me on this point—that you messed up, Carl."

"I tried," he said.

"Of course, you tried," Davey said, switching the knife into his right hand. As he did so, Carl's flashlight caught the blade at such an angle that Carl momentarily blinded himself with the reflection of his beam. Davey went on. "But whereas Tom feels it was a matter of too little, too late, I feel it was a question of too *much*, too late."

"I d-don't understand!" Carl stuttered.

"Tracie," Davey said. "How does Carl feel to you right now?"

"Fine," she said.

"Are you sure he doesn't feel a bit cold?"

"He feels fine," Tracie said. "Make your point and be done with it. We're not your pets."

"You might want to stand back from your beloved while I make it," Davey said.

"Stop it, Davey," Cessy said firmly, although apparently she was not going to be leaping to anyone's rescue. She continued to stand near the doorway, as if she were guarding it. Davey glanced back at her.

"Shut up," he said.

Cessy didn't respond. Davey turned back to them. Tracie hugged Carl tighter. "We've done nothing to you," she said.

"What do you mean, I did too much?" Carl demanded.

Davey smiled. "You drowned, too."

"No," Carl said, shaking. "That's not possible."

"You washed down here," Davey said. "We got a hand on you but you slipped away. I'm sorry, Carl, but you're as dead as Joe."

Carl stepped back, pushing Tracie aside. He did feel cold then. He felt as if a flood of ice water had poured over his body for one whole year and washed away everything he called his own, including his soul. Yet he had to protest.

"I don't believe you!" he cried. "You lie!"

"True," Davey said, raising his knife. "But this doesn't."

Davey plunged the knife deep into Carl's chest. Carl tried to scream and couldn't. Davey pulled out the knife. It was covered with blood.

But Carl felt no pain. The knife had not hurt him.

Davey laughed joyfully. "Run, Carl. Try to get away from us again. See if we don't catch you. This is the part of the hunt we've all been waiting for."

Carl turned and ran.

CHAPTER
XII

In the Church

THE BOY FINISHED HIS STORY AND FELL SILENT. ON THE other side of the screen, the priest leaned forward, the smell of alcohol still strong on his breath. The boy wished he could see the man's face.

"Then what happened?" the priest asked.

"I ran," the boy said. "I ran all the way here."

"Then this mine is not far from here?" the priest asked.

"I told you, it's not a mine," the boy said. "It's some kind of tunnel these creatures carved into the earth."

"Millions of years ago?"

"I can't be sure about that. They lie about everything."

"Would you be willing to take me to this place?"

"No! I'll never go back there."

"But if I came with you, and we brought along a police officer with us," the priest said. "You would be safe."

"You haven't heard a thing I've said. Guns can't stop them. They move like lightning. They have the strength of a dozen men."

"Even the girl?"

"She's as bad as he is."

The priest thought about it for a moment. "What do you want me to do, son?" he asked finally.

"I want you to help me!"

"How?"

"I don't know. You're a priest. These things have come back from the dead. Doesn't the Bible have anything to say about things like them?"

"Not to my knowledge."

"Look, they're obviously related to snakes and lizards. The devil is always portrayed as a serpent. There's got to be a connection." The boy stopped. "What was that?"

"What was what?" the priest asked.

"That sound?"

"I didn't hear anything."

"Listen." The boy strained his ears, but nothing came back to them. He wasn't certain if he had heard anything to begin with, if it hadn't simply been a shift in the air.

As if a door had been opened?

He was in a church. They couldn't get him in a church.

"Never mind," the boy said.

The priest shifted away from the screen, his shadow blurring on the translucent material. "Did they really kill the young man?" he asked.

The boy bit his lip. "Yes."

"And these are friends of yours from school?"

"No. Well, yes, in a way. But they're not people. You've got to understand that by now, for Christsakes."

"Don't swear."

"I'm sorry."

"Who did you murder?"

"No one."

"But you've been saying you murdered someone all night?"

"I know I sound confused. I am confused. I'm not sure if it was murder. I don't think it was, but they act like it was. When they say something, and they have their eyes on you, it's hard not to believe them. I tried to save him. I really did. But—"

"But what?"

"Nothing."

"But they say you tried and died?"

The boy swallowed. He needed a drink almost as much as he needed to breathe. Yet when he thought of water, any water, he felt sick to his stomach. He glanced about the tight confines of the cubicle and thought of the miles of black walls he had traversed to reach the open air. He touched his chest and thought of the blood dripping from the knife.

"Yes," he said miserably.

"Do you believe them?"

"Why do you keep asking me these questions?" the boy cried. "You're the priest! You tell me if I'm dead or if I'm alive!"

"Oh, you're alive. I can assure you of that."

The boy sat back. "Thank you."

"But I don't think you're well."

The boy paused. "What do you mean?"

"I think you need help. More than I can give you tonight."

"You mean, you don't believe me?"

"I believe some of what you've said. But this stuff about people coming back from the dead and a civilization of reptiles millions of years old—that's pure fantasy. You should know from your schoolbooks that that's impossible."

In a single leap, the boy was as furious as he was frightened. The old drunk had just been humoring him!

"My schoolbooks?" the boy said. "You have a lot of nerve. You believe a man once turned water into wine. Do you know what my schoolbooks would say about that? What kind of priest are you anyway? You're always talking about the devil. Well, here I've brought you one. No, I've brought you two. You should be happy!"

"It's late," the priest said. "And I have to be up early tomorrow morning for mass. Now I can have someone at the directory give you a ride to the nearest . . ." The priest's voice trailed off. "What was that?" he asked.

"I didn't hear anything," the boy said. The words were no sooner past his lips, however, when he did hear it—a faint knocking noise accompanied by an even fainter scraping sound.

Oh, God, no.

"Is someone there?" the priest called out. "Hello? Someone is there." The shadow of the priest stood. "Excuse me, son, I will be back in a moment."

"No!" the boy cried. "Stay where you are!"

The priest did not heed his warning. He opened his confessional door, a door even his ancient scriptures could not have warned him to keep closed.

"What are you people doing here?" the priest demanded. "You can't—"

The boy bowed his head and closed his eyes. He didn't try his door, even though there always existed the possibility Davey would have allowed the priest to go free had he not been denied what he had come for. Yet the boy did not believe it. Davey was going to be denied nothing he desired, and what he desired most was to kill. Also, the boy was too frightened to move.

The priest began to scream.

It was a horrible way to end, in pain and terror. But the priest did not scream long before he began to choke. The boy heard the thrash of wild kicking, the tearing of material, the sounds of futility. The noise seemed to go on forever. Finally, though, it came to an abrupt halt with a soft thud upon the floor. Davey had let the body drop.

The boy opened his eyes.

A puddle of blood flowed under the confession booth door.

Someone knocked on the door.

"Carl," Davey called. "It's time to come out. The ceremony's about to begin."

CHAPTER
XIII

NEITHER TRACIE NOR PAULA WATCHED THE MURDER OF the priest. Davey accomplished the evil deed inside the cubicle set between the two confessional booths. But both girls knew how he did it. He had a thin steel wire stretched taut in his hands when the priest made the mistake of opening his door.

Thirteen-year-old Cindy Pollster found garroted.

An old favorite, no doubt.

Cessy stood behind them during the execution, as calmly as if she were waiting for a prankish younger brother to finish letting the air out of a friend's tire. Neither of the girls appealed to Cessy to stop Davey. They could no longer speak. Besides having a sharp knife and a bag full of supernatural abilities in his back pocket, Davey also had a roll of duct tape. He had shut them up for the time being. Tracie wished he had put some wax in her ears while he had been at it. The poor man—Davey took his time killing him.

Tom was outside during the execution, searching behind the church for Carl. Davey had sent him on the errand, undoubtedly knowing full well Carl's precise location. Tracie found it interesting that Davey did not want Tom around when he killed. Hiking back up the tunnel, they met Tom at approximately the half-way point, and when Tom asked where Rick was, Davey replied that they'd have to go back for him later when they weren't in such a hurry. Naturally, Tracie and Paula's mouths had been out of service long before then and they weren't able to correct the misinformation.

Rick. Such a great mind. Such a beautiful heart. How could he be gone? Yet Tracie was making no effort to try to accept the loss. She would not grieve till Davey had been destroyed. And destroy him she would, she swore it. He was going to burn.

Tracie remembered well Mark Sanders's remark in the diary.

"I don't believe they care much for fire."

Plus Cessy had stopped Paula from lighting her cigarette, almost in fear. They had to be vulnerable to fire. But Cessy had not taken away Paula's lighter, and now Tracie had it. She had slipped it from Paula's shirt pocket while they had pursued Carl across the sand in the truck. She had to plan her move. Their overconfidence in their superior strength and speed was a weakness. They had bound their mouths, but not their hands.

Tracie was visually searching the church for something flammable when Davey emerged from his sport with the priest. In his bloody right hand he had a bottle of tequila.

Probably more than a hundred proof, this far south.

She wondered if she could ask Davey for a hit of the booze before he slit her throat. It might appeal to his perverse sense of humor. Then she could club him with it and soak his clothes in alcohol and torch him.

Yeah, if he slows down by a factor of ten.

That was a problem. A big problem.

Cessy cleared her throat. Tracie glanced over her shoulder at the witch. Their eyes met. It was silly how none of them at school had realized earlier that these two did not belong. They never blinked. Plus their blue-black pupils were perpetually dilated. On the other hand, there was something magnetic in those eyes. Dark as pits they were, but also as mysterious as deep icy wells. Tracie started to turn away but hesitated. Cessy seemed to want to say something to her. That was why Cessy had cleared her throat—to catch her attention. But although Tracie thought she heard a question from Cessy, she could have sworn Cessy's lips hadn't moved a fraction of an inch. Nevertheless, somehow Tracie got the distinct impression Cessy was trying to tell her something about the bottle of tequila.

The bottle of water, Tracie. Water.

Yeah, that was right, Tracie thought.

But where was that bottle again?

Davey is holding the bottle. Water. Tracie.

Tracie wanted to ask Cessy to clarify the situation. There was only one bottle and Cessy was talking about two of them. Of course, there had to be two because one was water and the other was—well, it must have water in it, too. Wherever it was. Anyway, Tracie thought, with the tape over her mouth, she wasn't going to be asking Cessy anything.

The urge to question Cessy passed as quickly as it had come, and Tracie wondered what had brought it on in the first place. Cessy couldn't be worried about the bottle of water Davey was holding.

Tracie felt suddenly dizzy. But that, too, passed swiftly.

Davey banged on the confessional booth door.

"Carl. It's time to come out. The ceremony's about to begin."

Carl answered the summons. He was haggard and pale, but not shell-shocked like Paula, who was only going through the motions of being alive. She was walking. She was breathing. But there was nothing in her eyes. Tracie hoped she returned to her body soon. They might need her before this was all over.

Tracie did not believe for a moment that Carl was dead. It must have been a trick or an illusion with the knife. Davey lied as often as he smiled, which was almost constantly.

Carl glanced down at the priest. The top of the man's bald head pressed open the door a couple of inches. Carl was standing in his blood.

"I'm glad you've been to confession," Davey said. "Now you might stand a chance to get into heaven."

"Why did you let me go in the first place?" Carl asked.

"Why did we have the scavenger hunt?" Davey asked rhetorically and laughed. "For fun! You should know by now. There's no purpose to anything we do."

"But you say you need your sacrifices," Carl said bitterly.

"Oh, but that's where the fun comes in," Davey

said. "Look at you, Carl. You're ready to pee your pants. But imagine this." Davey held up his bloody wire. "Soon you may have nothing to put in those pants." Davey motioned over his shoulder. "To the altar."

They followed the side aisle to the front of the church. Davey directed Tracie and Paula to sit in the pew to the left of the polished brass tabernacle, where the altar boys probably rested their feet during mass. The place was beautiful, with a shiny brown marble floor and an intricately sculpted ten-foot-tall wooden crucifix. Just their luck that Cessy and Davey were lizards and not vampires.

There were candles everywhere.

Davey set the bottle he carried on the edge of a wide holy water bowl located near a statue of the Virgin Mary, and rolled up his sleeves.

"Doesn't quite have the sting of back home," he remarked as he washed the blood from his hands, referring to the holy water. Midway through his freshening up, he paused to smell the bottle and poured a couple of gulps into the bowl. A quart size—it had plenty left when he was through with it. But Tracie did not understand what was so special about the bottled water that he would go to the trouble to add it to the bowl.

A factor of ten?

What did that relate to? Tracie couldn't remember.

Cessy sat on the wooden divider that circled the altar, her long tan legs swinging easily, her big dark eyes on Carl. He stood on the altar not far from the cross. He wouldn't even look at her.

The door at the rear of the church opened and closed. Tom strode stiffly up the central aisle. "I couldn't find him," he said.

"Well, that's OK, since he's here," Davey said, drying his hands on the gold linen sheet that covered the top of the tabernacle. Davey took Mr. Partridge's sunglasses from his back pocket and handed them to Tom. "Why don't you put these on, Joe," he said. "And let everyone have a good look at you."

Despite all that had been said beneath the ground, Davey meant the remark as a revelation, and indeed it was. Their combined views of the universe were slow catching up with the combination of all they had witnessed. These monsters came back from the dead. By now, that was an established fact, beyond debate. Why, then, after all they had seen and heard, was it so difficult to accept the possibility that a friend of theirs had also come back? Tom was Joe. It was very simple. He didn't look the same as Joe had. He didn't even act the same. Tom was like a Joe that had taken too many hard drugs. Plus they *remembered* Tom as a separate person from Joe.

Yet that was the big lie. There was no Tom in any of their memories. There was only the pain of Joe's leaving, and the wish that he could return. And perhaps that was how Davey made such easy believers out of all of them. They wanted to believe—at least a part of the lie.

Paula's eyes widened at Davey's remark. She was back in her body.

Carl took a step toward his old friend. "Is it you, Joe?"

Tom lowered his head. He had not put on the glasses. "You've always known," he said.

"This can't be," Carl whispered, shaking his head.

"I wasn't that easy to forget, was I?" Tom asked quietly.

"I didn't forget you." Carl paused, going very still. "It *is* you."

"I'm the best one to explain this," Davey said, stepping between them. He loved an audience. "Lately, it's been harder for Cessy and me to get back over here. Not many people have been dying in this neck of the woods. Thousands of years ago, we didn't have that problem. We had rivers and lakes out here, and the Indians were always killing each other for the least little thing. They'd die furious, wanting revenge. We'd get them in the perfect frame of mind. That was how Joe came to us. The last thing he had on his mind when he drowned, Carl, was how you cheated him of his life. He died wanting to get even with you. We need that sort of *in* to do our stuff—unfinished business you might call it. It's this that allows us to come back, and it's our annual sacrifices in Valta that allow us to stay here. We made a deal with Joe. We'd fix him up inside a body, we said, and in return he'd help me get elected class president." Davey grinned. "Now I'd call that a bargain."

"But I didn't cheat you," Carl told Tom.

"I remember differently," Tom said, looking up, a spark of life crossing his face. "It was your idea to try to cross the gully. I didn't want to cross it."

"I wanted to cross it because there was higher ground beyond," Carl said. "There was a cave we could have taken shelter in. How the hell could I know

188

that that accursed spot was going to send a goddamn flood down upon us?"

"Watch your language," Davey said. "This is a church."

"All right," Tom said, his tone heating up, and it was as if he were coming alive for the first time. "You made a mistake. What about when the water came and dragged me off? I called to you for help. A hand from you and I could have been saved. But what did you do? Nothing! You just climbed farther up the embankment and stood there and watched me drown!"

"That's not true," Carl said.

"I saw you!" Tom said. "I saw you with my two eyes!" He glanced down at the glasses in his hands, lowering his voice. "When I had two eyes."

Carl hesitated. "I did stand there and watch for a few seconds," he admitted.

"A few seconds," Tom said. "It may as well have been a few hours."

It was Carl's turn to bow his head. "I'm sorry."

"Sorry," Tom said bitterly. "A lot of good that does me now." He glanced at the tall cross. "It's only right you should die in my place."

Carl looked at Davey. "According to this bastard, it's already too late for that."

Davey pulled out his knife. "Got this from a special effects man in Hollywood." Davey demonstrated how the blade slid into the handle and then sprang back out covered with red gook. "He had a half dozen of them in his collection. He showed them all to me. When he was done, I stuck this one in his stomach. Surprised him, it did, that I had the strength to keep the blade out." He eyed Tracie. "You might have read about him in the paper."

"So I'm not dead?" Carl asked.

"Not yet," Davey said.

"I want to get this over with," Tom told Davey. "We have to go back to the chamber room."

"For the transfer?" Carl asked.

"Yes," Tom said. "I live and you die. The scales will be balanced. You deserve it."

"For what?" Carl said bitterly. "I made a mistake in judgment. I hesitated for a few seconds. But I didn't murder you. I know I didn't, even though this *thing* has been doing his best to try to hypnotize me into thinking I did. I tried to save you, Joe. I ran after you along the ridge that overlooked the gully. I found this long pole. I held it out for you to grab."

"I remember none of this," Tom said.

"Because you were already losing consciousness," Carl said.

"Then how was I supposed to grab your pole?"

"When I saw that you were not responding to my calls," Carl said, "I threw down the pole. I dived in after you."

"You're saying you risked your life to save me?" Tom asked.

"Yes. I almost drowned, too. I was dashed against a boulder. I split open my side. I broke three ribs."

"I don't believe you," Tom said, shaking his head.

Carl took a step toward him and tore open his shirt. Along the right side of his well-muscled torso lay a twisted scar. "It took twenty-five stitches to close. By the time I got to a doctor, I had almost bled to death. I was in the hospital for a week." He let go of the shirt and touched Tom's arm. "I tried, Joe, I really tried. You just got away from me."

All this was obviously new to Tom. Or Joe. Tracie didn't know how to think of him. He considered a moment before responding.

"I still don't believe you," Tom said. "Davey was watching from the other side. He saw you run away and save yourself."

"Davey," Carl said sarcastically. "Who is he? *What* is he? He's a murderer and he's a liar, we know that much. Look what he did to Rick."

"Rick?" Tom asked Davey.

"He's fine," Davey said, waving a hand. "We'll get him later."

"Rick's dead," Carl said. "These two murdered him. They snapped his neck and shoved him through that door into the acid."

"We snapped his neck?" Davey said, throwing his sister a look.

"Do you feel strong?" Cessy asked her brother.

Davey jumped toward her. "What did you do?"

Cessy shrugged. "What could I do?"

"And Davey murdered that priest over there," Carl said. "See the body? See the blood? He's evil, Joe."

Tom was confused. "Rick can't be dead. That was not the deal."

"You can't deal with him," Carl said. "He's a witch. He casts spells. Look at me. This whole school year, I saw you every day, but I didn't recognize you. You were an old friend. You were even my best friend. But you weren't Joe. I saw you but I didn't see you. He took part of the truth and twisted it in my mind. Look at you, Joe. When you were alive you couldn't hurt a fly. Now you're talking about sacrificing your best friend. Look what he's done to you!"

"Did you hurt Rick?" Tom asked Davey.

"No," Davey snapped, glaring at Cessy.

"But that priest," Tom said. "Who killed him?"

"I did," Davey said, turning away from Cessy. "He tried to kill me. You know how these priests are. They're all drunks."

"Where's Rick?" Tom insisted.

"He's in the chamber room," Davey said. "You'll see him when we return."

"Yeah, you'll see him all right," Carl said. "You'll see his bones. Don't you know why he's bound the girls? They know the truth. If you don't believe me, ask Paula. Ask your girlfriend, Joe."

Tom had to think again. It appeared he did so against heavy resistance. Davey had his hypnotic eyes on him again. Yet Tom looked Davey straight in the eye when he said, "I'm untaping their mouths."

"Go ahead," Davey said. He glanced at his watch.

Tom set about removing the duct tape from their mouths, and more than a few hairs from the back of their heads. While he worked, his hand brushed Tracie's cheek, sending a chill to her bones.

He was *cold*.

"Where is Rick?" he asked, stepping back when he was finished.

"Dead," Tracie said.

"Paula?" Tom asked.

How did Paula feel? How could she feel sitting

before the ghost of her true love? Tears soaked her eyes, but even though her hands and arms were free, she did not reach out to hug him. She nodded mutely at his question. Tom whirled on Davey.

"You lied to me!" he cried. "You weren't supposed to kill Rick."

"Tom," Davey asked, his tone bored. "Do you have any idea how many I have killed since you helped me back here? No? Neither do I. Of course I lied, you fool. You *human*. Why would I do anything to preserve any of you?"

Tom drew back, his face choked with fury, gathering his strength. Then he leapt, and what followed next happened so fast that Tracie couldn't follow it. But when it was done, Tom lay in a ball of agony on the floor of the altar, his lower right leg bent at a cruel angle.

"Seems all that time in the desert sun has made your bones brittle," Davey said, standing over him. "Don't worry. We'll set it straight as soon as we peel away your flesh." He kicked him hard in the gut and Tom gasped in pain. "Your second death will be much slower than your first."

"Don't do that," Cessy said.

Davey looked up. "Why shouldn't I?"

"Because I like Tom," she said.

"Did you like Rick?" Davey asked, mad.

"Oh, yes," Cessy said, a dreamy tone to her voice. "He was a wonder."

"What are you talking about?" Davey asked impatiently.

Cessy climbed to her feet and began to stroll about

the altar, taking in the statues, the stained glass overhead, the smell of incense and the flicker of the candles. She drew in a deep breath, her whole body seeming to throb with sensation.

"These humans have begun to interest me," she said. "They have such a variety of feelings and thoughts. They've created customs we never had a chance to develop."

"I thought all you cared about was their food," Davey said.

"And their drink?" Cessy asked with a smile, picking up the bottle, tilting it to her lips, and swallowing a thick mouthful. "This is good. It's all good. But I've tasted it all before. I wanted something new this time. I wanted something I could bring back."

"You're beginning to sound like one of them," Davey said.

"Perhaps," she said, still holding onto the bottle.

"You've destroyed more of their kind than I ever did."

"Did I?" Cessy asked, her eyes floating about the church, finally coming to rest on the tall wooden cross. "I don't remember. I suppose I did. It seems I was another person then."

"What did you do with Rick?" Davey demanded.

"I destroyed him. Feeling weak, brother?"

"No." Davey checked his watch again. "But we've got to get back to Valta. Which one should we use?"

"Which *one?*" Cessy asked, surprised.

"Which two. We haven't much time if we're to stay."

Cessy shrugged. "I don't care."

Davey was shocked. "You don't want to sacrifice?"

"I don't care." Cessy glanced at the statue of the Virgin Mary. "Who is she, Carl?"

Carl wouldn't speak to her. Tracie stood quickly. "She was the mother of Jesus Christ," she said. "He was supposed to be the son of God."

"I've heard of him," Cessy said. "Your stories say he had powers such as ours." She nodded to the shrine. "What do you do with the candles?"

"You light them and then you say a prayer," Tracie said. "You're supposed to receive a blessing in return."

"A blessing?" Cessy asked, her eyes falling upon her. Tracie had never realized before exactly how big they were, how dark. Or perhaps she'd had the realization before, but it had been long ago. She couldn't remember, not for sure, but staring into Cessy's eyes, she had the same sensation she'd had while descending deeper and deeper into the tunnel, coming closer and closer to that horrible hell.

"A special favor from God," Tracie said.

"God? Which one is he?"

"God isn't a person," Tracie said. "He's our creator. He's the one who made us. He's the one who made you."

"But we have no God," Cessy said.

"Oh," Tracie said, suddenly finding it hard to think, to even see clearly. A thin translucent layer of black was settling over her vision, as if she were not only looking into Cessy's eyes, but looking out them as well. The colors of the church changed for her, becoming paradoxically richer and flatter at the same time.

She could see far more detail, yet she could not *feel* what she saw. The translucent layer was like a hard plate of glass, keeping everything at a distance.

"This is foolishness," Davey said.

"Why did you say he made us?" Cessy asked, ignoring him.

"There is supposed to be only one God," Tracie said.

"And this is his mother?" Cessy asked.

"The mother of his son," Tracie said.

"Had she powers?" Cessy asked.

"I believe so," Tracie mumbled. Why couldn't she look away? And what was Cessy saying? There were her words, of course, but that wasn't half of it. Tracie felt as if she had two streams of consciousness in her mind. The usual one, flowing effortlessly forward with her own thoughts, and this other, stagnant like a cesspool caught in a swamp of stinking plants, yet powerful, too, with the weight of a primordial ocean hidden beneath it.

And an erupting volcano standing behind it.

Tracie saw fire. All-consuming. Filling her brain.

"I would like to light a candle to this mother," Cessy said.

"Why?" Davey asked, wary.

"To feel this blessing," Cessy said.

"It is an empty custom," Davey said.

"It may have a power of its own," Cessy said, giving him a calculated look that seemed designed to heighten his distrust. "If you are afraid, you need not experience it."

As Cessy's eyes moved to her brother, Tracie felt a lessening of the spell, and was finally able to recognize it for what it was. Yet a portion of Cessy's being remained inside her own. The fire continued to blaze. The gaze into Cessy's eyes had left her with a taste of the creature's real power. Tracie's flesh vibrated with a strange intensity. She felt that if she really wanted, she could fly.

At Cessy's suggestion of his cowardice, Davey grew more annoyed. "You have been difficult lately," he said.

"Have I?" she asked, mocking.

His face was cold. "Remember who brought you here."

"Remember who I am," Cessy said, equally cold.

He flinched at the remark. "It's getting late."

"I want to feel the blessing," Cessy repeated, and the desire sounded blasphemous coming from her. Her eyes strayed to Paula, focusing on her now, though she continued to speak to her brother. "Will you join me?"

"Yes," Paula whispered, so faintly Tracie doubted even Davey could have heard her. Davey gestured to the cross and the statue.

"They were only human like the rest," he said. "They're dead."

Cessy pointed to Christ. "I heard this one came back."

"A fool would believe it," Davey said.

"We were fools long ago," Cessy said, her cold eyes still glued to Paula, the bottle still in her right hand. "I wonder."

Why does she continue to hold that bottle?

The reason hovered at the edge of Tracie's mind, but it would not come inside.

"What do you wonder?" Davey demanded.

Cessy was long in answering. When she finally did, though, she turned away from Paula and gave her full attention to Davey.

"I wonder," Cessy said, "what you are afraid of."

"Are you all right?" Tracie whispered to Paula.

"I am," Paula said, with unexpected firmness.

"I fear nothing," Davey said.

"This is not your place," Cessy said. "You don't have to join me."

Davey considered a few seconds before nodding and taking a step forward. "I have an eye on you," he warned.

"That is good," Cessy spoke to Paula and Tracie. "Assist us."

They gathered about the shrine to the Virgin Mary. Tracie and Cessy stood closest to the statue, with Davey and Paula a few feet behind. Carl had gone to help Tom, who was sitting unmoving on the marble floor before the shiny tabernacle, holding on to his broken leg. Cessy had finally set the bottle down, to their right, on the divider that enclosed the altar. Tracie lifted the stick used to light the candles.

"It's a simple ceremony," Tracie said, unsure of what she was demonstrating, or why. "We light a candle and we say a prayer."

"A prayer?" Davey asked, showing faint interest. "You mean, an invocation?"

"We usually say the Hail Mary when addressing the prayer to the Virgin," Tracie said, not understanding his question.

"Then what?" Davey asked impatiently.

"She has already explained," Cessy said. "Then we receive a blessing."

"The Virgin's especial providence is to aid those in trouble," Tracie said, wondering if the words were her own. Cessy's close proximity had her thinking as well as seeing double again. As Cessy surveyed the rows of burning wicks, the lights reflecting clearly in the depths of her flawless blue-black eyes, Tracie saw an ancient continent ablaze with rivers of incandescent lava, pouring forth from countless volcanoes thrust up from the depths of the earth. And Tracie knew she was seeing the ruin of Cessy's civilization as Cessy had seen it, knowing also that Cessy had been young when the cataclysm struck.

Young and hungry.

"Nonsense," Davey said.

"Shh," Cessy said. "Say your prayer, Tracie. Then say one for me and light your candles."

Tracie began. "Hail Mary, full of grace, the Lord is with thee. Blessed art thou amongst woman, and blessed is the fruit of thy womb, Jesus. Holy Mary, mother of God, pray for us sinners, now and at the hour of our death. Amen."

Finishing, Tracie lit a candle and then repeated the ritual once more, from start to finish. The second time around, though, she did not have Cessy in mind. She was trying to push her out of her mind. She was beginning to pick up the fumes from the long-dead volcanoes, not with her nose, but from deep inside her brain. The smell resembled that at the purple house and in the black chamber. It wasn't real, but it was still making her sick to her stomach. As Tracie lit the second candle, Cessy looked over at her and smiled. Cessy knew what she was trying to do, and didn't care. Cessy knew nothing was going to push her away.

"Do you feel protected?" Davey asked sarcastically.

"Yes," Cessy said slowly. "You must try it."

Davey did not want to get too close to the candles. He had Paula handle the stick. Nor did he want to take his eye off Cessy. He kept her near the shrine, close to him. Despite Davey's remarks, he appeared curious about the ceremony. Since he employed a ceremony to stay alive, it was understandable. Perhaps he feared his sister might gain a power he did not possess. Having been dead a hundred million years, Tracie thought, he had to be superstitious. Cessy seemed to be using the Catholic ritual as a bait of some kind. But for what purpose, Tracie did not understand. Tracie retreated several feet to the right, behind the three of them, folding her hands at her back.

Her fingertips brushed the bottle sitting on top of the divider.

She glanced at it. She read the label.

Tequila.

That's what it was! How could she have forgotten?

The bottle of water, Tracie. Davey is holding the bottle.

Cessy had forced her to forget it was tequila! But why? Tracie gripped the neck of the bottle with her right hand, feeling the same strange power of a moment ago, her earlier resolve for vengeance returning like the tidal wave of a desert flood. She stared at the back of Davey's head.

"This ceremony cannot work," Davey said. "It has no victim. It's foolish, I tell you."

"Shut up," Cessy muttered.

"What did you say?" Davey asked, as Paula waited with the burning stick in her hand. Yes, waiting, Tracie thought, for a sign.

"I told you to shut up," Cessy said.

"You would dare?" Davey asked, his tone deadly.

"You shouldn't have killed my dog," Cessy said, not looking at him, staring straightforward at the statue.

"This will not be tolerated," Davey said, shaking with anger.

"I liked that dog," Cessy went on. "And you shouldn't have forced me to kill Rick. I liked him, too."

"He was human!" Davey said. "He was nothing!"

"He was my friend," Cessy said. "And you shouldn't have made me your lover. You're not my friend." Cessy finally turned toward him, and the cold light that blazed from her eyes could have pierced a wall of stone. "In fact," she said, "I don't even like you. I don't think I've ever liked you."

Davey stopped. His anger left him. He smiled. He began to chuckle. "I will close the door on you."

Cessy smiled, too. "I will lock it on you." She glanced at Paula. "Say your prayer, girl."

"I don't know it," Paula said. "I'm not Catholic."

"It doesn't matter," Cessy said. "Where I come from, there are no prayers. There are no blessings. There is no God. We protect ourselves. Or we perish." She lowered her voice. "Protect yourself."

The sign.

Tracie lashed out with the bottle. Her speed almost snapped her arm off at the socket. Her reflexes were ten times that of normal. Cessy definitely still held a portion of her mind and body. Yet it was not a control. Tracie was in complete control. It was an amplification.

The bottle exploded over the back of Davey's head, the tequila drenching his shirt and pants. But it did not knock him out. He whirled upon Tracie, his face unrecognizable. The blow had in no way injured him, but no human being could have twisted living flesh into such an expression of pure hatred and been called human. His was the face of the lost creature that lay hidden inches below the surface of the world's last undiscovered cesspool, preserved in unrelenting misery through a hundred ages, waiting for its day.

Tracie recoiled in horror.

It was Paula's turn. Cessy had prepared her equally as well. In a blinding flash she snapped the candle lighter toward the wet shirt Davey presented to her as he turned. Unfortunately, Davey was as crafty as he was old. The first attack had alerted him to further attacks. Before Paula could touch the flame to his clothes, he spun through another half revolution and knocked it from her hand and into the altar boys' pews.

"You lose, *sister,*" he whispered to Cessy, raising a dangerous hand.

She did not respond, except to hold his eye one last time.

A knife plunged deep into Davey's back.

"Joe wanted me to give this to you," Carl said, twisting the blade deeper before pulling it free. The composition of Davey's blood matched the black trail at the purple house. The blade literally dissolved in Carl's hand, and he was forced to drop it before the acid consumed the handle as well. Davey fell to his knees on the hard marble floor, hugging his chest in agony.

"Cessy," he gasped.

"I never lose, *brother,*" Cessy said.

"When I first got here," Carl said to Paula, pointing to the shrine, "I lit that candle and prayed."

Paula quickly lifted it. "This one?"

"Yes," Carl said.

"I'm glad it was answered," Paula said. She touched the flame to the top of Davey's head.

The fireball engulfed his body in an instant. As a group they jumped back, none quicker than Cessy. Screams followed, and although Tracie heard in them the sweet sound of revenge, she wished she had not had to hear them at all. Like his many victims before him, Davey did not go quickly or pleasantly.

Yet unlike them, he ignited before he died.

Tracie stomached only quick glances of the spectacle. At first Davey was a thrashing ball of flames. Then the fire seemed to get sucked inward, drawing fuel from his internal organs rather than his clothes and the oxygen in the air. The surrounding temperature shot upward as the flames soared swiftly through the spectrum of color, from orange to yellow to blue, searing into a blinding purple that brought forth from Davey a high shrill note that held within it as much surprise as it did pain. Maybe he was seeing God at last, and God was not pleased.

There followed a loud pop. A ten-foot-tall ten-thousand-watt lightbulb could have exploded inward. The fire went out. A brief torrential wind swept the church. Stained glass windows shattered. The candles died.

Then all went silent, and a darkness, usually found only far underground, settled over the church.

EPILOGUE

An undetermined length of time passed. It may have lasted seconds, or several minutes. Carl did not know. He was not even sure if he was still alive. He could neither see nor hear anything. It was not until Tracie flicked on her lighter that he began to get a grasp on the situation.

Quickly Tracie relit several of the candles in the shrine to the Virgin Mary. In the soft orange glow, the first thing Carl noticed was Cessy bent over Tom. She was rubbing his leg with her hands, and it was straightening out, becoming whole. It was not long before she was able to help him to his feet. They watched in awe, for it seemed to them a miracle that a deathless monster should also have the power to heal.

The marble of the altar was badly scorched, but of Davey there was not a trace.

"Is he gone?" Tracie asked.

Leading Tom slowly toward the light of the shrine, Cessy nodded. Of them all, she alone remained unruffled. Indeed, the old playful glow had already returned to her cheeks, and she was once again the Cessy whom Carl had admired and desired for so long. Yet, in another sense, the illusion was shattered forever for him. How could it be otherwise? She was a lizard, for godsakes.

"He's gone, and he won't be coming back," Cessy said.

"How can you be sure?" Tracie asked.

"He could only enter this world through the door of Valta," Cessy said. "He could only exit that way if he was to have any hope of returning. It has always been that way."

"Is it the same for you?" Tracie asked.

"Yes," Cessy replied, and she flashed a dangerous smile. "But don't get any ideas."

"Did you use us to help destroy him?" Tracie asked.

"I felt that, too," Paula said quickly.

"I gave you the opportunity to help yourselves," Cessy said. "But had it not been for Carl, whom I did not help except to hold Davey steady for a moment, you would all have been killed."

"Why did you pluck the idea of using the tequila from my mind?" Tracie asked.

"Davey has never been able to sense minds the way I can," Cessy said. "Still, he might have become aware what you were thinking."

"Did you *need* us to kill him?" Carl asked.

"Davey could never have harmed me," Cessy said. "He has never understood who I am. I could have destroyed him with a thought."

"Then why didn't you prevent him from killing Rick?" Tracie asked.

"I did not know Rick and you girls would come to the chamber room," Cessy said. "He tricked me. You see, that room is his special place, and the secret of returning to this world has been his special knowledge for a long time. It was a knowledge that I didn't have until recently. He would have been hard to stop in that room. But here he was vulnerable. I counteracted his use of Rick in the ritual. Davey did not learn that until he arrived here. That's why I kept asking him if he was feeling strong. I enjoyed telling him he was running out of time." She added, "Not that any of this could have affected me. I could have challenged him in the chamber room and beaten him. But none of you would have survived such a challenge."

"Then why didn't you at least save the priest?" Carl asked.

"Why should I have?" Cessy asked innocently.

"Did you really kill Mark Sanders?" Tracie asked, disgusted, and not afraid to show it.

"I've killed thousands," Cessy said. "Their names never mattered to me." She glanced at the shrine, and a faint note of wanting to be understood entered her voice. "I need victims to remain here. Where I come from—you would not call it a pleasant place."

"Why the farce of the scavenger hunt?" Carl asked.

"It was Davey's idea," Cessy said. "He felt it would slowly heighten your fear, and thus serve his need for tension. I see now, though, he used it to bring extra victims to Valta, more than he required." She shrugged. "He enjoyed torture. It was a hobby of his."

Tracie pulled a handful of newspaper clippings

from her back pocket. "Is this what all these murders were about?"

"Yes," Cessy said. "When we sacrifice, for a purpose, it is always done in Valta, and only once a year."

"But even with these sacrifices," Carl said, "it seems your time does eventually run out."

"Yes," Cessy said.

"What are your hobbies?" Tracie asked.

Cessy smiled again. "They have been many and varied. I am also known to your history by a number of names."

"Recent history?" Carl asked.

Cessy stopped smiling. "No."

"Why did you help us, Cessy?" Carl asked.

"I wonder myself," she replied, turning her back on them and picking up one of the tiny red dishes that held a lit candle. They might have assumed—after all they had witnessed—that the flame posed a peculiar threat to her. That is, until she put it out with her bare fingers.

"I said earlier that nothing changes," she continued. "And that has been true for me. I have walked in your world a thousand times. I have tasted every physical pleasure you can imagine, and many you cannot. But lately they have all begun to taste the same to me. I must be bored. I bore easily. Although our race was old by your standards when it destroyed itself, it was also very young. We were like children. Spoiled. Impatient. Quick to anger. That is why Davey and I settled in your high school. We wouldn't have fit in your adult world."

She turned toward them again, and it could have

been the somber light, but a delicate line of sadness seemed to touch her brow. "But since this century began, I have wanted more. I have wanted the subtle pleasures that you humans can bring each other." She paused, and her luminous black eyes went to Tracie. "Do you love Carl?"

Tracie flushed. "Why do you ask?"

"I have watched you," Cessy said. "I have sensed things in your mind that are alien to me, which are both sweet and painful at the same time. They come upon you whenever you think of Carl. I would have that sweetness, if I could, and even the pain it brings. Could you tell me about it?"

"I don't know what to say," Tracie mumbled, lowering her head.

"Please?" Cessy said.

Tracie glanced at Carl. He felt embarrassed for her, but also glad. He wondered how he could have been so blind to her feelings. Suddenly, he felt the warmth inside her as clearly as he had felt the coldness beyond the arched doorway. The love was directed at him, and even though a monster had been the first to show it to him, he had a feeling he would not lose sight of it for a long time to come.

Tracie could have been the mind reader Cessy was. She smiled at his thoughts of her.

"My love for Carl is the greatest power in the universe," she said, no longer ashamed. "It's a blessing from God."

"Him again?" Cessy said, puzzled. "Who is this God?"

"You really don't know?" Tracie asked.

Christopher Pike

"No."

"But you've been on the other side?" Tracie asked.

"There are many sides to that door," Cessy said. "There are many doors on this side. You go through some, we go through others. It is seldom we meet in the place where I met Joe. It is just as well for you. It is a hard place." Cessy glanced over at Tom. "We have to go now."

Tom shook his head. "Not with you."

She raised a surprised eyebrow. "We had fun."

"It's over," Tom said firmly.

Cessy shrugged. "As you wish."

Tom felt no need to reply. Cessy turned to leave. Paula stopped her, going so far as to touch her.

"But what about my brother?" she cried.

"He's dead," Cessy said.

"Bring him back!"

"I can't."

"But you have powers. You can heal. Why can't you restore him to life the way you did Joe?"

"I have told you," Cessy said patiently. "I counteracted Davey's use of Rick in the ritual. Rick is not bound to Valta, and therefore he is beyond my reach."

A tear ran over Paula's cheek. "But I miss him."

"Rick's body was weak," Cessy said. "He was tired of his chair. More than anything, he wanted to travel. He had a rich imagination. He wanted to see the whole universe." Cessy smiled and wiped away Paula's tear. "Why do you weep? Now he is free to go wherever he wishes. Maybe even to visit this God your friend keeps talking about."

"He didn't suffer?" Paula asked.

"He didn't even know what hit him," Cessy assured Paula, touching her finger. Paula looked down at it in surprise, then flexed it without pain. Carl assumed Cessy had healed it as well.

Again, Cessy turned to leave. Carl stopped her this time. He didn't grab her, though, not in a million years.

"There's something I don't understand," he said. "When you woke me this morning, I was dreaming. Did you know that?"

"Yes."

"Do you know what I was dreaming about?"

"Yes."

"Who was the monster?" he asked.

She smiled. "The future."

"I don't understand?"

"Now my time runs low," Cessy said. "But I know the secret of the door. I will be back. And when I do return, I'm going to look you up, Carl." She glanced at Tracie. "I'm going to find out about this *love.*"

Tracie came down the steps of the altar and took his arm.

"Don't bother," Carl said, squeezing Tracie's hand.

Cessy chuckled. "You say that now. But when that time comes, you'll be old, and sick, and worried about dying. You'll welcome me with open arms."

"Don't count on it, sister," Tracie said.

Cessy was not impressed. "You'll be old, too, girl, and nothing to look at." Then she suddenly moved forward and kissed Carl on the lips before he could turn his head, using her immense strength to press her warm mouth to his ear and pull him away from Tracie. "When that time comes, you won't recognize me," she whispered. "But for the present I'll give you a clue you may want to remember. I'm going to offer to take you swimming. And I'm going to allow you to *look* all you want."

She released him and turned and strode toward the back door. She was gone before they realized it.

"Bitch," Tracie said.

"She has her points," Carl said.

Tracie shoved him in the side. "You have weird taste in women."

He pulled her back to his side. It felt good to have her there. "You're right," he said.

Paula was saying goodbye to Joe. Yes, Joe, not Tom. Davey's hypnotic spell on him was done with.

"You have to leave, too?" she asked, sad.

"I have to stay," Joe said. He glanced toward the dead priest. "It's you who have to go."

"But what will we tell people?" Carl asked.

"The less the better," Joe said.

Carl understood what he was saying. Davey's body had vaporized. There were no outside witnesses to testify what had befallen the priest. Indeed, they could walk out of the church this second and leave it all behind them. Except for Rick. That was going to be hard to explain, but perhaps they could get away with playing stupid. He's gone, they could say, we don't know where. And it would be the truth.

"But that place," Carl said. "It must be closed down."

Joe shook his head. "Don't go back there. Don't even go near it."

"But?" Tracie began.

"Listen to me," Joe said.

"We will," Carl said.

"Will you find Rick?" Paula asked, another tear on her cheek.

"If I can," Joe said.

The immensity of what she had lost, and what she was losing, hit Paula again. She fell into his arms, grabbing him. "But you can't go! I can't lose you again, Joe, I can't. I'll die. I've spent this last year dying without you."

Joe hugged her in return. "You never let go of me because I never let go of you. I came back, Paula, and it was a sin. It doesn't matter that we didn't talk this year, or that you hardly looked at me. I looked at you. I've watched you since Davey brought me back. And a part of you knew I was watching. That's the part that's been killing you." He held her at arm's length. "But that's done with now. I will go one way and you will go another. I'm sorry, but it's the only way it can be."

"No," she moaned, clenching her eyes shut, crying.

"Yes," Joe said gently. "You must go. Now. Please. Before I try to stay."

"You could?" Paula asked, opening her eyes, a faint note of strained hope in her voice.

"Don't tempt me," Joe whispered.

Her head fell, and in the gesture Carl saw she understood what her boyfriend meant, what it would cost for him to remain, the lives that would have to be sacrificed. It was too high a price for anybody to pay, even for love. In resignation, still crying, Paula pulled Joe's gold chain over her head. There was only one of them now. The other had disappeared with Davey, like the fool's gold. She placed it around Joe's neck.

"I haven't taken this off since you left that night," she said.

"I know," Joe said, touching the chain.

"You'll remember me?" Paula asked.

"I'll remember."

"Forever?"

Joe kissed her briefly. "We may yet have that together."

There was much Carl wanted to ask his old friend. Did he believe him? Did he forgive him? Would he also remember him? But the time for many words had passed, and they were unnecessary. Joe turned to him and they hugged, and in the embrace Carl felt a lifetime of warm memories that would live for both of them even when life was over.

"I loved those hikes we used to take together," Joe said when they let go of each other. His face was calm, and a clear light shone behind his eyes.

Carl nodded. "I hope someday we can do it again."

Somewhere, he meant. But it was left unspoken—and it was better that way. Leaving Joe, they turned and walked toward the back door of the church, stepping outside onto the hard stone porch, feeling the faint crunch of desert sand beneath the soles of their shoes. The night sky was ablaze with the light of the moon. A soft breeze rich with a sweet fragrance blew across their faces. All was calm.

"Was this a dream?" Tracie asked.

Carl peeked one last time into the church. The candles burned alone. The altar was empty. He let the door close.

"No," Carl said. "We're never going to wake up and forget this night." He thought of Cessy's last remarks and shivered. "Never."

Look for Christopher Pike's
Fall into Darkness

About the Author

CHRISTOPHER PIKE was born in Brooklyn, New York, but grew up in Los Angeles, where he lives to this day. Prior to becoming a writer, he worked in a factory, painted houses, and programmed computers. His hobbies include astronomy, meditating, running, playing with his nieces and nephews, and making sure his books are prominently displayed in local bookstores. He is the author of *Last Act, Spellbound, Gimme a Kiss, Remember Me, Scavenger Hunt, Final Friends* 1, 2, and 3, and *Fall into Darkness*, all available from Pocket Books. *Slumber Party, Weekend, Chain Letter, The Tachyon Web,* and *Sati*—an adult novel about a very unusual lady—are also by Mr. Pike.